A Word from Stephanie about Writing the Perfect Love Letter

There are two things every romance needs: a girl and a boy. But what happens when two girls get involved with the same boy? Disaster! At first, it seemed so simple. My best friend, Darcy, liked this boy named Max. No problem, right? Wrong! Because Darcy liked Max so much that she was too nervous to even speak in front of him. And when she tried to write him a note, she couldn't think of anything to say. So Darcy begged me to help her out.

And I said yes. All I had to do was write a few love letters to Max—and sign Darcy's name. It was simple—until I realized the awful truth. *I* liked Max, too! And Max liked the girl who wrote him love letters. But who were the letters really from? I was writing them. But Darcy's name was on each letter. So which one of us was Max's true love? And how would my friendship with Darcy ever survive this mix-up?

I'll tell you all about it. But first I want to tell you about something that *isn't* mixed up: my family. My very big family.

Right now there are nine people and a dog living in our house—and for all I know, someone new could move in at any time. There's me, my big sister, D.J., my little sister, Michelle, and my dad, Danny. But that's just the beginning.

When my mom died, Dad needed help. So he asked his old college buddy, Joey Gladstone, and my Uncle Jesse to come live with us, to help take take care of me and my sisters.

Back then, Uncle Jesse didn't know much about taking care of three little girls. He was more into rock 'n' roll. Joey didn't know anything about kids, either—but it sure was funny watching him learn!

Having Uncle Jesse and Joey around was like having three dads instead of one! But then something even better happened—Uncle Jesse fell in love. He married Rebecca Donaldson, Dad's co-host on his TV show, *Wake Up, San Francisco*. Aunt Becky's so nice—she's more like a big sister than an aunt.

Next Uncle Jesse and Aunt Becky had twin baby boys. Their names are Nicky and Alex, and they are adorable!

I love being part of a big family. Still, things can get pretty crazy when you live in such a full house!

FULL HOUSE™: Stephanie novels

Available from MINSTREL Books

FULL HOUSE™
Stephanie

My Secret Secret Admirer

Diane Umansky

A Parachute Press Book

READING

A MINSTREL® BOOK

Published by POCKET BOOKS
New York London Toronto Sydney Tokyo Singapore

A MINSTREL PAPERBACK *Original*

 A Minstrel Book published by
POCKET BOOKS, a division of Simon & Schuster Inc.
1230 Avenue of the Americas, New York, NY 10020

A PARACHUTE PRESS BOOK

 Copyright © and ™ 1997 by Warner Bros.

FULL HOUSE, characters, names and all related indicia are trademarks of Warner Bros. © 1997.

ISBN: 0-671-00363-1

First Minstrel Books printing October 1997

10 9 8 7 6 5 4 3 2 1

A MINSTREL BOOK and colophon are registered trademarks of Simon & Schuster Inc.

Cover photo by Schultz Photography

Printed in the U.S.A.

My Secret Secret Admirer

CHAPTER
1

◆ ◀ ◆ ◆

"Late again!" Stephanie Tanner declared, glancing down at her watch.

It was a Wednesday afternoon in September, and Stephanie stood where she always stood at 2:35 P.M. on school days. At the pay phone outside the gymnasium of the John Muir Middle School.

Every afternoon Stephanie met her two best friends, Allie Taylor and Darcy Powell there. But for the past few weeks, Stephanie had been *meeting* Allie and *waiting* for Darcy.

"I know. Darcy is constantly late!" Allie complained, shifting her leather backpack from one shoulder to the other. "And I have a piano lesson at four. You know how Ms. Schroder is. If I'm late, she'll make me play 'Greensleeves' at double speed!"

"Well, they don't you call Flying Fingers Taylor for nothing," Stephanie joked. She had been friends with Allie since kindergarten, and she knew Allie didn't do *anything* at double speed— eat, talk, or play the piano.

In fact, Allie was the calmest person Stephanie knew. She even looked sort of calm, with reddish-brown hair that waved softly down her back to her shoulders. Today she wore it in a high ponytail tied up with a green scrunchie that matched her eyes.

Stephanie checked her watch again: 2:40 P.M.

"Come *on*, Darcy," she grumbled, pushing her straight blond bangs out of her eyes.

Darcy had been friends with Stephanie and Allie since sixth grade, when her family moved to San Francisco from Chicago. She was as energetic and talkative as Allie was calm and quiet. And Darcy put her high energy to good use. She played lacrosse and tennis, and whatever other sport caught her interest.

Lately, though, even Darcy couldn't keep up with her own schedule.

"It's that field hockey team," Stephanie declared. "Ever since Darcy became captain, she's practically been a walking, talking hockey stick!"

2

Allie laughed.

"It's true," Stephanie insisted. "Darcy is working so hard at field hockey! That's why she's constantly late. Even *before* practice, she's always talking to the coach and trying to come up with some amazing new way to get a goal."

As soon as ninth grade had started, Darcy was named captain of the junior varsity hockey team. Stephanie was really proud of her best friend. But lately she was beginning to think hockey was taking over Darcy's whole life!

"Let's leave her a note," Allie suggested, digging into her backpack for a pen and paper.

"Steph! Allie!"

The gym door next to the pay phone burst open. Darcy raced out the door toward her friends. She wore a short blue kilt, an orange and blue jersey with the word "captain" across the front, baggy gray knee socks, and large white shin pads. Her thick black hair bounced as she ran.

Darcy waved a piece of paper in the air. "Check this out!" she exclaimed.

Darcy's dark brown eyes flashed with excitement as she shoved the paper in front of Stephanie and Allie. It was the latest copy of *The Scribe*, the John Muir Middle School newspaper. Stephanie was a staff writer for the paper.

"Do you know anything about this?" Darcy asked breathlessly. "*Anything?*" She pointed to a front-page article with the headline "John Muir Ninth-Grader Launches Park Cleanup Program."

Stephanie glanced at the article. "Sure," she replied. "I saw it before it was even printed. It's about a new program to clean up Reese Park. You know, that place down by the river."

Allie nodded. "Of course—we went there all the time when we were little. Remember when we used to swim in the Reese Park pond every day of the summer, Steph?"

Stephanie smiled. "It was the best. But you can't swim in that pond now—it's really gross. The whole park is a mess. So some John Muir kids are forming a committee to clean it up. There's a meeting tomorrow for volunteers."

"Should we go?" Allie asked.

"Wait a minute!" Darcy cried. "Forget the park for a second. That's not what I meant. Do you know anything about *him?*"

She placed a slim finger on the picture right next to the article. Stephanie peered down at the photograph. It showed a boy with thick, straight blond hair; a small, freckled nose; and big brown eyes rimmed by the longest lashes Stephanie had ever seen. He wore a bandanna tied around his head.

"Well?" Darcy demanded excitedly.

"I know who he is," Stephanie answered. "That's Max Halsey."

"Max Halsey," Darcy repeated. A wide grin spread across her face. "More," she insisted. "Tell me more. Do you know anything else about him? I've got to know!"

Stephanie shrugged. "I don't know much," she told Darcy. "But he's supposed to be pretty cool. I think he's really into the environment. Oh, and I heard that he tutors kids from Bridge Elementary School."

Allie nodded in agreement. "I heard that too," she said. "And I saw Max at the recycling center when my dad and I went to drop off papers. He was working there—I think as a volunteer."

"Max Halsey," Darcy said again, leaning against the pay phone with a dreamy smile on her face. She held *The Scribe* in front of her and gazed at Max's picture.

Stephanie and Allie exchanged puzzled looks.

"Why are you so interested in Max, anyway?" Stephanie asked.

Darcy folded her arms around her copy of *The Scribe* and hugged it to her chest. "Because I think he's totally cute," she announced. "I like him. I mean, I *really* like him. And I have to meet him! Do you think he has a girlfriend?"

5

Stephanie pulled her hairbrush from her backpack. "I don't know. But I've never seen him with a girl," she replied.

"Me neither," Allie added.

"Awesome!" Darcy cried. She spun around, making her kilt fly in a circle. "Well, what do you think? Am I the perfect girlfriend candidate for Max?"

"But you don't even know him," Stephanie pointed out, running her brush through her hair.

Darcy grinned. "I don't know Max *yet*," she agreed. "But I will soon. And then I'll let him know that I like him. Simple."

Darcy is so confident, Stephanie thought. *She probably* will *meet Max. And she'll probably walk right up and talk to him.*

"Excuse me, Darcy, but exactly *how* are you planning to let Max know that you like him?" Allie asked.

"Hmmm." Darcy bit her lip thoughtfully. "I know!" she cried. "I'll send a singing telegram to his house!"

Stephanie and Allie giggled.

"How about a personal radio announcement?" Stephanie asked. She spoke into her hairbrush, pretending it was a microphone. "This just in. KZOB has learned that Darcy Powell likes Max

Halsey. We repeat, Darcy Powell likes Max Halsey. Details at eleven."

"I know!" Allie said with a grin. "How about hiring a pilot to write your message in the sky?"

Darcy laughed. "That *would* get his attention," she declared.

"And everyone else's in San Francisco," Allie joked.

Stephanie squinted down the hall—and spotted a tall blond boy wearing a bandanna around his head. "Uh, Darcy?" she said. "Don't look now. But I think you're going to get your chance to meet Max sooner than you thought."

"Huh? What do you mean?" Darcy asked. Her voice suddenly sounded nervous.

"He's walking right toward us," Stephanie whispered. "With Paul Petronio, that guy from the soccer team."

Darcy gasped. "Toward us? Max? Oh, I can't believe it," she murmured. "Now I'm nervous. Really nervous. Oh boy. Oh boy."

"Here he comes," Stephanie reported. "Come on, Darce. This is the perfect opportunity to meet him."

"Yeah," Allie added. "Just say hi or something."

Darcy nodded. "I know, I know," she replied. "I just didn't expect this."

Darcy took a deep breath. "Wish me luck," she whispered as Max and Paul walked closer and closer to the phone booth. She put on a big grin and stepped directly into Max's path.

He was only two feet away.

Talk to him, Stephanie urged her friend silently.

Max was right in front of Darcy.

Now, Darcy, Stephanie thought. She expected Darcy to say something funny and original, the way she always talked to boys.

But then something strange happened.

Darcy's big grin shrank into a timid little smile. She turned away from Max and glanced at his friend Paul.

"Hi, Paul," Darcy said to the dark-haired boy. "How's soccer going?"

"Great," Paul replied with a grin. "On your way to hockey practice?" he asked. He gestured at Darcy's uniform.

Darcy nodded, keeping her eyes locked on Paul. "Got to keep practicing!" she declared.

Why is Darcy talking to Paul? Stephanie wondered. *She's completely ignoring Max!*

Paul smiled as he and Max walked past Darcy. "Well, keep up the good work," he said over his shoulder. "See you around."

"Yeah. See you around," Darcy replied, still smiling her timid little smile.

Darcy stared at the boys' backs as they walked out the double doors to the school's driveway.

Then she sank down to the floor and leaned against the cinder-block wall. "I blew it!" she moaned. "I'm a major wimp. I didn't even say hello to Max."

"Darcy, what happened? Why didn't you talk to him?" Stephanie asked. She and Allie stared down at their friend in confusion.

Darcy shook her head, as if she didn't understand it herself. "I just couldn't," she mumbled. "I guess I have too much of a crush on him."

Stephanie studied her friend thoughtfully. Darcy looked miserable. All the shine and sparkle had disappeared from her eyes.

"Wow," Allie said. "This is serious, Darce. You really fell for this guy, huh?"

Darcy nodded sadly.

Stephanie hated to see Darcy so unhappy. "Don't worry, Darcy," Stephanie declared. "I know who can help."

Darcy gazed up at her with a spark of interest in her eyes. "Who?" she asked hopefully.

Stephanie pointed to herself. "Stephanie Tanner—Crush Doctor!" she cried. "By the end of this month, Max will be completely in love with you—guaranteed!"

CHAPTER
2

"Come on, you guys! Hurry!" Darcy called down the hall on Thursday afternoon. The end-of-school bell had just rung.

Darcy tapped her sneakered foot impatiently. "We've got to get to the pizzeria and grab a good table!"

"Check it out—Miss Always-Late is early for once," Stephanie whispered to Allie as they hurried toward Darcy. "Do you think the fact that we might run into *Max* at Tony's Pizzeria could have something to do with it?"

"Hmmmm, let me think," Allie replied with a giggle. "I think you might be on to something there, Steph!"

Tony's was one of Stephanie's favorite hangouts—all the kids from John Muir went there. Besides the best pizza in town, Tony's also had mini-jukeboxes at every table and awesome video games.

"What took you so long?" Darcy complained as Allie and Stephanie walked up. "I've been waiting forever!"

"Darcy, the bell just rang a couple of minutes ago," Stephanie pointed out.

"A couple of minutes? For your information, the bell rang at least . . ." Darcy checked her watch. "Oh, three minutes ago. Sorry. I guess it just *felt* like forever!"

Stephanie smiled at her friend. "Why are you in such a rush to get to Tony's?" she teased. "Is it the pizza—or Max?"

Darcy grinned. "I think it's both," she said. "Of course, I don't know for sure that Max will be there. But I'm hoping! This is the only day I don't have hockey practice for the next week."

She twirled around in front of her friends and smoothed her hair. "Do I look okay?"

"Perfect!" Stephanie told Darcy, checking out her bright yellow T-shirt and black and white checked mini-jumper.

Darcy took a deep breath. "Okay, then I guess I'm ready. Let's go."

The girls hurried down the hall and pushed

open the school door. They ran down the steps and made their way toward Tony's Pizzeria, about four blocks away.

Darcy stopped outside the door. "Do you think Max is in there?" she asked. She stared at Stephanie and Allie with wide, nervous eyes. "You guys look. I can't. I just can't!"

Stephanie pressed her face to the window and tried to peer through the glass. But the sun's glare made it impossible for her to see anything inside Tony's.

"Stephanie, stop!" Darcy cried. "Max will see you looking!"

Quickly, Stephanie turned away from the window. Darcy grabbed her arm. "Did you see him? Is he in there?" she asked.

"Darcy, relax. I can't even see inside," Stephanie said. "And so what if Max sees me looking through the window? Come on. Let's just go in and have a slice."

Darcy took a deep breath. "I have to get a grip," she said, running her hand through her thick hair. Then she pulled open the door. "You guys go first," she told Stephanie and Allie.

Stephanie walked into Tony's and looked around for a few seconds. Her friend Anna Rice waved from a booth near the jukebox. The Flamingoes—a group of snobby girls from school—

sat at their regular table in the back of the room. Familiar-looking John Muir kids filled the rest of the booths and tables.

"Boy, this place is really packed!" Stephanie declared.

"Max? Did you say you see Max?" Darcy asked in a panicky voice. "Where is he? Where?"

Allie and Stephanie exchanged glances. "*Packed*, Darcy. I said this place is really packed," Stephanie corrected her.

"Oh." Darcy breathed in relief.

Stephanie grabbed Darcy's arm and steered her toward the counter. "We'd better get this girl some pizza—and fast," Stephanie told Allie.

"What'll it be?" asked John, the cook. He tossed a disc of dough up into the air.

Stephanie ordered a soda and a slice with extra cheese. Allie asked for a plain piece. Then Darcy took her turn. "A slice with triple pepperoni, garlic, and sausage," she told John.

"Gross!" Stephanie cried, wrinkling her nose. "Darcy, I don't know how you come up with your combinations."

"It's awesome," Darcy said as John set the pizza on the counter. "Maybe I'll even let you taste it."

"No thanks," Stephanie replied, picking up

her slice. "Come on, that booth on the side is empty. Let's grab it."

The three girls walked to a booth right across from the counter—and right next to the door. Stephanie and Darcy sat down facing the entrance. Allie slid into the seat across from them.

"This will be excellent," Darcy declared. "We can see everyone who comes in."

Darcy brought her brimming slice of pizza toward her mouth. She bit into it hungrily. Stephanie lifted her slice too, ready to bite into the hot cheese.

The door opened—and Max strolled into the pizzeria, followed by Paul Petronio.

Stephanie elbowed Darcy, who was concentrating on her pizza. "Darce, it's Max," she whispered. "And he's looking over here."

Darcy, startled in mid-bite, nearly dropped her slice.

Oh, no! Stephanie thought. *Darcy is going to dump pizza in her lap—right in front of Max!*

But at the last second, Darcy caught the slice and kept it from falling.

Whew! Stephanie thought. *That was close.*

Just then, the huge pile of cheese and toppings on Darcy's overloaded pizza began to slip—right off the dough! Darcy gave a little yelp, and crammed the whole mess into her mouth.

Her mouth was totally stuffed with pizza!

Horrified, Stephanie glanced at Max.

He was staring right at Darcy!

Then Max turned away, and he and Paul stepped up to the counter. Darcy's face turned bright red with embarrassment.

This is awful, Stephanie thought. *I have to help Darcy!*

"Come on," Stephanie exclaimed, setting the rest of her slice down. She pulled Darcy and Allie to their feet and led them to the counter, where Max and Paul were waiting for their food.

"Back so soon, girls? What can I get you now?" John asked.

Stephanie gently pushed Darcy up to the counter, right between Max and Paul.

Darcy gulped, chewed, and swallowed, her face still bright red. "Um, I'll have another Darcy special, I guess," she blurted out.

Then she turned to Max.

She stared at him with wide eyes. He stared back at her.

Come on, Darcy, Stephanie thought. *Say something to him.*

Darcy's lips quivered nervously. She opened her mouth. As if she were going to speak.

But no sound came out.

Darcy quickly turned toward Paul. "So, did you catch the latest Schwarzenegger movie?" she asked.

"Yeah—it was awesome," Paul answered with a grin. "The way he destroyed those aliens with his laser-beam eyes—too cool!"

Paul opened his hazel eyes as wide as he could and imitated the actor. " 'You are dust!' " he declared in a fake Austrian accent. "What do you think?" he asked eagerly. "Do I sound like Arnold?"

"Definitely." Darcy giggled. "You're ready for Hollywood!"

Stephanie stared at her friend in amazement. *Why is she talking to Paul again?* she wondered. *Why doesn't she say anything to Max?*

As if she could read Stephanie's thoughts, Darcy turned back to Max. "Uh, you're Max, right?" she mumbled.

Max frowned in confusion. He looked as if he wasn't sure exactly what Darcy was asking him—or why. "Well, I was Max the last time I looked," he replied.

John slapped Darcy's pizza on the counter. It looked gigantic—piled about three inches high with pepperoni, sausage, and smelly cloves of garlic.

Darcy stared at her gigantic pizza slice and

burst into high-pitched giggles. In a few seconds her giggles turned to loud hiccups.

"Hic! *Hic!*" Darcy gasped. Her eyes flew open wide in surprise.

Do something! Stephanie told herself. She had to help Darcy.

"Um, I'm Stephanie, this is Allie, and you probably know Darcy," Stephanie said quickly to Max and Paul. "As you can see, Darcy has a good sense of humor."

"Hic! Hic!" The hiccups were even louder now.

"A really good sense of humor," Stephanie added. "Oh, yeah, this girl loves to laugh. Really loves it."

Stephanie slapped Darcy on the back to try to stop the hiccups.

"Hic! Uhhhhhhh." Darcy began making coughing, choking sounds.

"Water!" Stephanie cried. "We need water!"

John quickly filled a cup with water and set it on the counter.

Stephanie grabbed the cup and held it up to Darcy's mouth. "Hold your breath and drink," she urged. "That will help."

Darcy gulped some of the water down, red-faced with humiliation.

17

Max and Paul stared at Darcy. "Is she okay?" Max asked Stephanie.

Darcy nodded as she drank the rest of the water, still coughing a little.

"She'll be fine," Stephanie assured them.

"Just fine," Allie added. She grabbed Darcy's arm and led her back toward their table.

"Well, then, see you around," Max said. He and Paul carried their slices toward the door.

"Bye!" Stephanie called after them. She picked up Darcy's overloaded slice of pizza and brought it to the booth. Her two friends were already sitting down.

Darcy was slumped on the bench with her face buried in her hands. Allie shot Stephanie a worried look.

"Darce?" Allie asked. "Are you okay?"

Darcy lifted her head. "What a disaster," she moaned. "Could I possibly have acted like more of a geek?"

"Don't be upset, Darce," Stephanie told her. "Max won't think you're a geek. Remember when I pushed Rick into the pool over the summer? He still liked me anyway."

Rick was the boy Stephanie had dated last summer. He had just moved to New York City with his mom, who was an actress. Stephanie still missed him.

"Yeah, but at least you knew how to talk in front of Rick," Darcy pointed out. "I can't even speak to Max."

"Why not?" Stephanie asked, ignoring her cold pizza. "You can usually talk to anybody! You were fine when you were talking about movies with Paul."

"Yeah," Allie added. "But you totally lost it when you tried to say something to Max."

"I know," Darcy replied, shaking her head. "It's easy to talk to Paul. He's just a friend. But Max is sooo cute—it just makes me nervous when he looks at me. I can't stand it. I really can't stand it."

"What am I going to do?" Darcy gazed at her friends in desperation. "Stephanie—you have to help me!"

CHAPTER

3

◆ ◀ ▸ ◆

"May I *peas* have your attention?" Joey Gladstone asked at dinner that night. He set a steaming platter of peas and corn on the table.

Stephanie's father, Danny Tanner, groaned. But Stephanie knew he secretly liked Joey's bad jokes.

Joey was Danny's best friend from college. He'd been living with the Tanner family for nine years—ever since Stephanie's mom died in a car accident. Joey moved in to help Danny take care of Stephanie and her sisters.

"That joke was pretty *corny*, Gladstone," joked Stephanie's uncle, Jesse. Uncle Jesse lived with the Tanners too. He shared the third floor of the Tanners' house with his wife, Becky, and their twins, Nicky and Alex. "You need to be *squashed!*"

Jesse and Joey were always cracking jokes. They had a radio show called *The Rush Hour Renegades*. Sometimes they practiced their material at the dinner table.

"I know one!" Becky put in. "Don't let Artie Choke! Get it? Artichoke?"

D.J., Stephanie's eighteen-year-old sister, groaned. "No offense, Aunt Becky," she said. "But don't give up your day job." Becky was Danny's co-host on *Wake Up, San Francisco*, a morning TV show.

"Yeah—Dad would be lonely without you there every morning," said Michelle, Stephanie's nine-year-old sister.

Stephanie spooned some hamburger casserole onto her plate. She was only half listening to the family joking. She couldn't stop thinking about what happened at Tony's that afternoon. *How can I help Darcy with Max?* she wondered. *I need a dating expert to give Darcy some advice.*

That's it! she thought suddenly. *I'm surrounded by dating experts—Becky and Jesse and Dad and Joey. Even D.J.! They've all done a lot of dating.*

Stephanie tapped on her water glass with her fork. "Attention! Attention!" she called.

Everyone stopped eating and stared at her.

"I'm taking a poll," she explained. "Here's the question: What do you do if a guy makes you so nervous that you can't act normal or even talk around him?"

"I don't know, Steph," Joey answered. "Guys never make me nervous!"

Everyone giggled.

"I'm serious," Stephanie insisted. "This is important!"

Danny stroked his chin thoughtfully. "Well, if you're too nervous to talk around a guy, you could do things he's interested in," he suggested. "Then you could talk about that activity with him. For example, if this guy happens to like cleaning, you could join the Cleaning Club."

Everyone at the table groaned. Danny was crazy about cleaning. His idea of fun was polishing the wooden windowsills until they shined like mirrors. Danny even belonged to the Cleaning-Appliance-of-the-Month Club!

"Dad, there is no such thing as a cleaning club," Michelle declared. "That's totally silly."

"I don't know, Michelle," Stephanie said thoughtfully. "Dad's plan just might work. *Without* the cleaning part!"

After dinner Stephanie plopped down on the living room rug, grabbed the phone, and dialed Allie's number. "I have an idea for Darcy—and I think it's going to work," she declared.

"Awesome!" Allie exclaimed. "Let me get her

on the other line. Hold, please, for Darcy Powell," she added in her best operator voice.

Allie's parents had given her three-way calling as a Christmas present the year before. The three girls used it a lot—practically every night.

Nicky and Alex sat near Stephanie on the rug, tossing a soft red ball back and forth to each other.

"Steph? Darcy?" Allie's voice clicked back on the line. "Are you guys both there?"

"On the line!" Stephanie replied.

"I'm here too," Darcy answered in a dull voice. "Your friend, the geek."

"Oh, Darce, don't say that," Allie cried.

"It's true!" Darcy declared. "I keep thinking about what happened in Tony's today. You know, I'm surprised I didn't just faint in front of Max. I can't say a word to him without doing something completely stupid! This is the worst!"

The twins' ball rolled into Stephanie's leg. She tossed it across the living room. Laughing, Nicky and Alex hurried after it. "Well, I took a Tanner family poll," she informed Darcy and Allie.

"You told everybody in your family what a jerk I made of myself?" Darcy demanded.

"No, Darce," Stephanie assured her. "I just asked them what they would do if a guy made them so nervous that they couldn't talk to him."

23

"Did they have any brainstorms?" Allie asked.

"My dad did. He said that you could do an activity that the guy is really interested in," Stephanie explained. "And then it would be easier to talk to him—because you could talk to him about that activity."

"What activity—cleaning?" Allie asked with a giggle.

Stephanie laughed. "How did you guess?" she replied.

"I have an idea for you too," Allie told Darcy. "I found this terrific article in *Grrl* magazine: '101 Ways to Get Him Interested in You.' "

"Well, I obviously need all the help I can get," Darcy declared. "What does it say?"

"Here's number thirty-six. 'Bake him home-made cookies from your favorite recipe,' " Allie read aloud.

"Forget that," Darcy said. "I'd probably burn down my house."

"Then how about number fifty-three? 'Carry his books home from school,' " Allie read.

"Lame. You guys live in different directions anyway," Stephanie pointed out.

"Yeah, plus I usually have practice after school," Darcy added.

"Okay, here's a cute one: 'Walk his dog for him,' " Allie read.

"We don't even know if Max has a dog!" Darcy cried. "What if Max is a cat person? I give up. This is totally hopeless. I'll never get to know him."

"Wait!" Allie cried. "Here's a really, truly good one. Number ninety-eight: 'Join the club that he belongs to at school.' "

"Hey, that's practically what my dad said!" Stephanie exclaimed. "So, my dad and *Grrl* both think it's a good idea. What do you think, Darcy?"

"Well, I don't think Max likes field hockey," Darcy replied. "And that's what I like best."

"Do you think Max likes tennis? Or lacrosse? You were pretty into those sports last year," Allie pointed out.

"Max doesn't seem like the tennis-playing type," Stephanie said. "Or the lacrosse type. He's more into the environment."

"It's no use." Darcy sighed. "I don't know anything about environmental stuff. And it would look too weird for me to suddenly show up at a meeting of the Save-the-Earth Club."

Stephanie lay back on the living room rug and stared at the ceiling. *Think,* she told herself.

"I've got it!" she cried. "The Reese Park cleanup!"

"The park cleanup?" Darcy asked doubtfully. "You think so?"

"Definitely!" Allie put in. "It's a great idea!"

"Max is in charge of it," Stephanie went on. "And there's a meeting for volunteers tomorrow afternoon. You've got to go! Then maybe you can get used to being around Max."

"You're right. It is a great idea," Darcy said. Her voice took on some of its old bounce and energy. "What should I wear? Maybe my jean skirt. The really faded one? With my purple T-shirt and . . ."

Darcy sounds like herself again, Stephanie thought happily.

"Wait!" Darcy cried. "I forgot! I *can't* go to the meeting. I have hockey practice!"

"Oh, no," Stephanie said. "That's awful!"

"You're always practicing. Couldn't you skip it for just one day?" Allie asked.

"No way," Darcy replied. "You know I'm the captain. That means I have to figure out strategies and decide who should play what position. And we're playing Cliffside Junior High in a couple of weeks. That's a really big match. We have to practice almost every day if we want to win!"

"Darcy, I know how important field hockey is. But this is the perfect way to get to know Max,"

Stephanie pointed out. "Maybe the *only* way. You could at least come to the meeting late—after hockey practice."

Darcy was silent for a few seconds.

"Are you still there?" Stephanie asked.

"I'm here," Darcy replied. "I was thinking. You guys are right. The cleanup meeting is the best way to get to know Max."

"So you're going to come?" Allie asked. "That's great!"

"I'll try to get there—late," Darcy answered. "I really will. But, Steph, you're a reporter. So you can go to the meeting for me!"

"*For* you?" Stephanie repeated.

"Yeah," Darcy said. "And you can talk to Max for me and find out if he has a girlfriend. Find out everything you can about him! Will you, Steph?"

"I don't know, Darce," Stephanie said slowly. "What am I going to do—interview him?"

"Just ask him a few questions," Darcy replied. "You know, the way you do when you're working on an article for *The Scribe*. Please, Steph?"

"But don't you want to find out about Max yourself?" Stephanie asked. "I mean, wouldn't it be better if *you* ask him all these questions?"

Darcy groaned. "But I can't do it! I can't even talk to him at all!"

"Well . . . " Stephanie said.

"You said you wanted to help," Darcy pleaded. "And a real best friend would do this for me."

Stephanie sighed. "Oh, all right," she agreed. "I'll do it."

CHAPTER
4

◆ ◂ ◗ ◆

"Let's get this over with," Stephanie joked on Friday afternoon. "Reese Park cleanup meeting, here we come!"

"It's more like, *Max*, here we come!" Allie said. "I feel like a spy!"

Stephanie pulled open the classroom door, and she and Allie peeked inside. There were already about thirty kids sitting at the desks.

Max stood at the front of the room behind a small wooden podium. He was studying a stack of papers in his hands. A slide projector sat on a cart next to him, and a screen for showing slides hung from the wall behind him.

"Come on," Stephanie said. "Let's grab seats in the front."

"Yeah," Allie agreed. "So we can really check Max out."

They found two chairs right in front of Max's podium.

"Okay," Stephanie whispered. "Here's what we want to find out. One—does Max have a girl-friend? Two—what kind of stuff does he like to do? Three—where does he hang out and who does he hang out with?"

"Right," Allie agreed.

Max cleared his throat. "I guess we're ready to start. Thanks for coming," he called out in a clear, confident voice. "It's great to see you all here."

Stephanie watched him thoughtfully. He had a lot in common with Darcy, she decided. They were both really self-confident and energetic. And they both had great fashion sense. Max looked adorable in his soft denim shirt and baggy jeans.

Oops! Stephanie thought. I'm *not supposed to be thinking Max is cute—that's Darcy's job!*

"Reese Park could be one of the city's best parks," Max was saying. "But it's a mess. Paul, could you please hit the lights?" Max gestured with a remote control that he held in his hand.

Paul snapped off the overhead lights. Max

clicked the remote. Everyone in the room gasped as an image popped up on the screen.

The slide showed a rusty, sagging swing set. The ground around the swings was covered with a layer of old soda cans and crumpled newspapers. The grass was full of weeds.

"That's awful," Stephanie whispered to Allie. "It used to be such a nice park."

"Right now the neighborhood kids can't play in Reese Park," Max explained. He clicked the projector remote again and again, showing slide after slide of the dirty, run-down park. "And there isn't another park near their neighborhood."

"That's true," Stephanie whispered. "It's the only park we could ride our bikes to when we were little."

"Yeah. Everything else was too far away," Allie agreed.

Everyone in the room stared in amazement as Max clicked through the slides. Stephanie leaned forward in her chair.

"But we can clean this up if we work together," Max continued. "So here's the plan. We're going to do a litter patrol—sort of a mini-cleanup—next Wednesday. Then, at the end of the month we'll have a major cleanup day. And I'm going to ask the city council for some money—to buy play equipment and plants."

Wow, Stephanie thought. *This is a totally awesome project!*

Max clicked to a slide that showed a beautiful, clean park with beds of bright flowers and sparkling new swings and slides.

"Here's a park cleanup that kids did in Sausalito last year," he explained. "Kids like us. We can do the same for Reese Park. So come help us with litter patrol next Wednesday. And sign up for a committee for the big cleanup. There's fund-raising, publicity, recycling, community relations—and plenty of other committees. We need your help!"

Max turned the projector off, and the lights came back on.

Stephanie jumped to her feet in excitement. "Come on!" she told Allie. "Let's go sign up!"

"Sign up—and get some information about Max," Allie reminded her.

"Oh! Right," Stephanie said with a smile. She was so excited about Max's speech that she had almost forgotten the real reason they were there—to help Darcy!

The girls hurried up to the podium at the front of the room, where Max was handing out clipboards. "Write your name and phone number and the committees you're interested in," he called out as kids clustered around him.

Stephanie took a clipboard from him. "Great speech, Max," she said. "What an amazing project!"

"Thanks," he replied. He gave her a big smile. "I hope you'll help."

"Definitely," Stephanie told him. "So, um, will your girlfriend be helping too?" she asked in an innocent voice.

Max shook his head. "I don't have a girl-friend," he said. "I mean, I have girls who are friends, but, well"—he shrugged—"I'm sort of busy anyway."

"Right," Stephanie replied. "I guess all this cleanup stuff would keep you pretty busy. Don't you play soccer too?" she asked.

"No, that's my friend Paul," Max said. "I like baseball better. I play with some of the guys from my neighborhood sometimes."

"Baseball," Stephanie repeated. She filed the information in her brain.

Max turned away and began talking to some of the other kids. Stephanie wrote her name and phone number carefully on the clipboard she was holding. Then under "committee interests" she jotted down "fund-raising and publicity." Allie did the same.

"Good work with Max," Allie whispered. "Hey, there's Darcy."

Stephanie glanced toward the classroom door. Darcy was rushing toward them, still wearing her field hockey uniform. She was sweaty, and her kilt was covered with dirt. But her dark eyes sparkled.

"I snuck out of practice for a few minutes," she murmured as she drew close to Stephanie and Allie. "But I've got to get right back. Coach will probably knock me down to team manager if she notices I'm gone!"

Then Darcy spotted Max, who stood bent over the slide projector next to the podium. "Look at him. He is so adorable," she whispered. "Totally adorable."

Darcy turned to Stephanie. "So?" she asked in a low voice. "What happened?"

"So he doesn't have a girlfriend," Stephanie whispered back. "And he likes playing baseball. And you're going to sign up for the publicity committee. Allie and I already did."

Allie handed the clipboard to Darcy, who jotted down her information.

"Why don't you go give the clipboard to Max?" Stephanie suggested.

"Give it to him?" Darcy asked. She glanced nervously over at Max. "I don't know—he looks busy."

"Go ahead," Stephanie urged. "That way he'll

definitely know you were here—at his meeting, sharing his interests."

Darcy nodded. "Okay. But come with me!" She grabbed Stephanie's sleeve and dragged her toward the projector cart where Max stood. He seemed to be having trouble pulling the slide tray out of the projector.

Darcy tapped Max on the shoulder. "Here, Max," she mumbled.

"He didn't hear you," Stephanie whispered. "Louder."

Darcy bit her lip. "Um, Max? Here's a clipboard," she repeated.

Max yanked on the slide tray—with no luck. "Darn!" he exclaimed. Then he glanced over his shoulder at Darcy.

"Oh, thanks," he said distractedly. "You can just stick it on the podium."

Stephanie pushed Darcy forward. "Talk to him," she urged.

Darcy swallowed nervously. Then she stepped up next to Max. "Boy, you're going to clean up a whole park," she said cheerfully. "I can't even keep my room clean!"

Max tugged on the slide tray again, hard enough to pull it out of the projector. "Finally!" he exclaimed. "Sorry—what did you say?" he asked Darcy.

Darcy gulped. "My, um, room's a mess," she stammered.

Max wrinkled his brow in confusion. He stared at Darcy blankly. "Oh," he finally said.

Darcy and Max looked at each other for a few seconds.

"Well, uh," Darcy stammered. She twisted a lock of her hair around her finger.

"Steph, *do* something," Allie whispered in Stephanie's ear.

Stephanie quickly stepped up to Max. "Darcy and Allie and I have an idea," she announced.

"What is it?" Max asked.

Stephanie glanced at Darcy. Her friend still looked too nervous to say anything.

"Uh, well," Stephanie began. "Darcy's, um, aunt belongs to the Parks Conservancy in Chicago. So *Darcy* thought maybe we should call everyone in San Francisco who belongs to the Parks Conservancy and ask them to donate money for playground equipment. Right, Darce?"

Darcy looked surprised. "Uh, yeah," she choked out. "Right."

"The Parks Conservancy people will already be interested in parks, so they'll probably give!" Stephanie finished.

Max grinned. "That's terrific!" he said. "Those

are the kinds of ideas we need, Darcy. We should talk more about it."

Darcy just stared at him.

"Yeah, Darcy has some other ideas too," Stephanie said.

Darcy shot Stephanie a panicked look. "Yeah, I think we, um, uh, should, er . . ." Darcy trailed off.

"Hey, Max!" Sheila Hall and Abby Gruby, two other ninth-graders, cut Darcy off in mid-sentence.

"Max, come over here," Sheila said, tugging on his arm. "We have a question about the recycling committee." She pulled him away.

Darcy kicked at the floor with the toe of her sneaker. "I did it again!" she moaned. "I try talking to Max and I act like a total loser!"

"It's not that bad, Darcy," Stephanie told her.

"Yes it is!" Darcy cried. "Steph, if you hadn't come up with that story about my aunt, I would've looked like a total jerk. I couldn't think of a single thing to say!"

Allie shot Stephanie a worried look.

"All I ever think about is Max," Darcy went on. "I can hardly eat or sleep, and I'm even messing up my hockey game thinking about him all the time! How am I ever going to get to know

Max if I can't act normal around him? How will I ever get Max to know the real me?"

Darcy glanced up at the clock on the wall. "Oh, great!" she cried. "Practice is probably over! Coach will be furious. What a horrible day!" Darcy turned and ran from the room.

Allie let out a sigh. "Poor Darcy," she said. "She's really upset about this."

"I know," Stephanie agreed. "We've just got to figure out a way to help her get together with Max!"

"We will," Allie said. "We'll think of something!"

Stephanie nodded. "But what?"

CHAPTER

5

◆ ◢ ◢ ◆

" 'All this time your letters—every one was like hearing your voice there in the dark,' " Stephanie declared. " 'I read them over and over. Every page of them was like a petal fallen from your soul.' "

That is so romantic, Stephanie thought. She stood in front of her English class on Monday, reading from a tattered paperback copy of *Cyrano de Bergerac*. She was playing the part of Roxane, a Frenchwoman of the 1800s who was in love with a soldier named Christian.

"You could even be *more* emotional," Mrs. Steiner, the English teacher, told Stephanie. "Imagine what's happening here: Christian has been sending these wonderful love letters to

Roxane. And now she's telling him how much those letters mean to her. She's expecting Christian to be able to *talk* to her as beautifully as he *wrote.*"

Stephanie nodded. She imagined Roxane reading Christian's letters, expecting his words to be even more wonderful in person.

"Okay, Christian," Mrs. Steiner said. "Let's have your next line."

" 'All this for a few absurd love letters?' " Bobby Fowler asked dramatically, kneeling down on one knee. " 'You felt that, Roxane?' "

"Great!" Mrs. Steiner said. "Now let's try putting this in our own words. Roxane, what would you say to Christian?"

Stephanie thought for a moment. "I guess I'd say 'Gee, your letters were so awesome.' "

Everyone in the class giggled. "And how would you reply, Christian?" Mrs. Steiner asked Bobby.

Bobby grinned. "I'd say thanks!" he replied.

Mrs. Steiner chuckled. "Thank you, Stephanie and Bobby. You did a wonderful job of bringing the characters to life. You can sit down now."

As Stephanie and Bobby returned to their desks, Mrs. Steiner stepped up to the blackboard. "Let's discuss what's happening in *Cyrano,* class," she said. "Christian loves Roxane. But he doesn't tell her to her face that he loves her—he *writes* to her instead. But there's a hitch. Who knows what it is?"

Raised hands waved in the air. "Cindy?" Mrs. Steiner said.

"Christian's friend Cyrano is the one who writes the love letters to Roxane!" Cindy Hartmann replied.

"And . . ." Mrs. Steiner prompted.

"And Christian passes them off as his own letters," Paul Murphy burst out. "So that Roxane will think he's a great writer and fall in love with him."

"Absolutely correct," Mrs. Steiner declared. "Christian asks Cyrano to help him win the love of fair Roxane—or Stephanie Tanner, in this case."

The class laughed.

"Now, why do you think Christian didn't just go and talk to Roxane himself?" Mrs. Steiner asked.

Larry Walls raised his hand. "He was afraid?" he asked.

"Right," the teacher said. "Christian was tongue-tied around Roxane. He could barely speak in front of her. He simply didn't know what to say."

41

Tongue-tied? Stephanie thought, startled. *That's what Darcy is around Max!*

That's it, Stephanie realized. It was the perfect plan! If Christian impressed Roxane with his love letters, maybe it would work for Darcy too. She could write Max a couple of notes. Then he'd get to know the real Darcy.

Stephanie barely heard the rest of Mrs. Steiner's lecture. *I can't wait to tell Darcy,* she thought. She's going to be totally psyched.

The moment the bell rang, Stephanie dashed from the classroom and raced down the hall toward the library. She, Darcy, and Allie had study hall this period.

Stephanie rushed across the library to the big round table in the back of the room. Darcy was already sitting there.

"Wait until you hear this!" Stephanie said, trying to keep her voice low. Mr. Mason, the librarian, was very strict about no one talking during study hall.

"Let me tell you my news first!" Darcy whispered back breathlessly. "It's awesome!"

"Cyrano!" Darcy cried.

"Cyrano!" Stephanie declared at the same time.

They stared at each other in amazement, and burst into giggles.

"I was in English class, and—" Darcy started.

Stephanie was so excited that she interrupted Darcy. "In English, we're reading—"

"Ahem!" Mr. Mason cleared his throat. "Quiet, please!"

"Sorry," Stephanie whispered, feeling a flush of embarrassment creep over her face.

She and Darcy tried to stifle their giggles.

"Are you talking about what I think you're talking about?" Stephanie asked, leaning in close to Darcy.

"Are you talking about what *I'm* talking about?" Darcy asked with a smile.

"What are you guys talking about?" Allie asked, setting her books down on the table. "I could practically hear you from the other side of the library!"

Stephanie took a deep breath and glanced around to make sure Mr. Mason wasn't watching them. "We're reading this incredible play, *Cyrano de Bergerac*, in English class," Stephanie explained.

Allie nodded. "So are we."

"Well, you know how Christian sends notes to Roxane because he can't talk to her?" Stephanie went on.

"That's the part my class is up to too!" Darcy

43

broke in. "And that's when I got the perfect idea—I can send notes to Max!"

"I thought of that, too!" Stephanie exclaimed. "That way, he'd get to know the real you."

"Definitely," Darcy agreed. "Not the nervous me who can hardly speak around him."

Stephanie nodded. "Right, because you wouldn't be talking to Max in person. At least, not until you'd written him a note—or two."

"You mean she wouldn't be *hiccuping* in person," Allie said with a grin.

Darcy gave Allie a playful pinch. "Don't remind me," she whispered.

Darcy dug into her battered plaid backpack. A button that read "Hockey Players Meet Their Goals" dangled from the zipper. She rummaged around for a few seconds, then pulled out a crumpled piece of notebook paper.

"There!" Darcy said. She smoothed out the wrinkled paper and set it on the table in front of her friends.

Stephanie and Allie bent their heads over the table to look more closely at the paper. "It's the start of my note to Max," Darcy explained. "I wrote a few things down right after class."

Stephanie squinted at the scribbled words on the paper. "Dear Max," she read. "You're a great gut—"

"Great guy," Darcy interrupted. She frowned. "I guess my handwriting is as lousy as my speech. I can't even make the *note* sound like I want it to sound!"

"Don't worry, Darce," Allie said. "We'll help you. Right, Steph?"

Suddenly Darcy clapped her hands. "Good idea! You can fix it, Steph," she declared. "You're just like Cyrano—a terrific writer. You're the best writer I know!"

"That's right," Allie put in. "You'll write the notes for Darcy, just like Cyrano de Bergerac!"

"It's a cool idea. Very romantic," Stephanie replied, drumming on the table with a pencil. "But the notes have to sound like *you*—so that Max can get to know *your* personality. Not mine!"

Darcy shrugged. "Well, then make it sound like me," she replied.

Stephanie raised her eyebrows. "How?"

"I don't know," Darcy answered. "You figure it out. You're the writer!"

"I have an idea," Allie put in. "Just pretend you're Darcy, and then you'll be able to *write* like Darcy!"

Stephanie looked at her friends doubtfully. "Do you really think we can pull this off?"

"Definitely!" Darcy said confidently. "You

know my personality better than anyone. I mean, you're my best friend!"

Stephanie smiled. "You're right. It will be no problem," she agreed. "In fact, it will be fun."

"You're the best friend in the entire universe! Well, you and Allie." Darcy cried, jumping up to hug Stephanie. "This will be great. Totally great."

Darcy gathered up her books. "I've got to fly," she announced. "Coach gave me a pass to go meet with her this period. We're going over plays for the game against Cliffside. I just wanted to tell you guys about the notes first."

"Wait, Darcy," Stephanie said. "What do you want me to say in the note?"

Darcy shrugged as she slung her backpack over her shoulder. "You're the writer, Steph," she declared cheerfully. "You'll think of exactly the right thing. I know I can count on you."

CHAPTER
6

◆ ◀ ◆ ◆

"I wonder what Cyrano de Bergerac would have for an afterschool snack," Stephanie said to herself. She was staring into the refrigerator. She couldn't wait to get started on Darcy's first love letter, but first she needed something to eat.

She pulled out the milk and poured herself a tall glass. Then she plopped a pile of chocolate-chip-nut cookies on a plate. She carried her snack up to the bedroom she shared with Michelle.

Stephanie grabbed a pen from her backpack and took a long, cold sip of milk. Then she rummaged around in her desk until she found an old note that Darcy had written to her. She wanted to imitate Darcy's handwriting when she wrote to Max.

She pulled out a sheet of the blue stationery Becky had given her for her fourteenth birthday, and plopped down onto the bed.

"Dear Max," Stephanie wrote as she chewed on a cookie. "You're as sweet as a chocolate chip cookie—and as nutty."

Stephanie frowned. *That is so lame,* she scolded herself.

She crossed our her first sentence. "Dear Max," she wrote. "When I saw you at the meeting, I really wanted to help clean up Reese Park."

Bo-ring, Stephanie thought. *But what else can I say? I know what I'd write. But what would Darcy say?*

Stephanie started again, this time glancing at Darcy's note to make sure she was copying her handwriting perfectly.

"How come you have that weird look on your face?" a voice asked from behind her.

"Huh?" Stephanie said, glancing up from the note. She was thinking so hard that she hadn't heard Michelle come into the room.

"Your face is all scrunched up. Like this," Michelle declared, wrinkling up her nose and pursing her lips. "How come?"

"I'm concentrating," Stephanie replied.

"Why do you have to scrunch up your face to concentrate?" Michelle asked.

"I'm writing a very important note for Darcy," Stephanie explained. "Well, it's for this guy named Max, actually. But we're going to pretend it's from Darcy. So it has to be in her handwriting."

"In *her* handwriting?" Michelle asked in amazement. "You can write in Darcy's handwriting? Isn't that hard?"

Stephanie shook her head. "Not really. It just takes practice," she replied. "Actually, it's sort of fun. Want to see?"

"Cool!" Michelle said. She jumped onto Stephanie's bed and sat facing her sister.

"Okay, here's Darcy's real signature, right?" Stephanie said, showing Michelle Darcy's old note. "First I trace it, so I can feel with my pen exactly how Darcy does it. Then I copy it about ten times until I've got it right."

Michelle's blue eyes opened wide. "That's unbelievable!" she declared.

Stephanie smiled at her little sister. "All right, that's the end of your handwriting lesson for today," she said. "I've got to finish this note."

Michelle stood up. "Okay. I've got to walk Comet soon, anyway," she replied. Comet was the Tanners' golden retriever.

As Michelle searched through the closet for her shoes, Stephanie picked up her pen again. "Dear Max," she wrote for the third time. She waited for a great thought.

But nothing came.

"Hey, what's going on?" D.J. poked her head into the room.

"Hi, Deej!" Michelle called. "Stephanie's concentrating."

"On what?" D.J. asked.

"Writing," Michelle answered.

"Actually, Steph, I came to tell you something cool about writing," D.J. said.

"What?" Stephanie asked.

"You know how I have to take creative writing at school?" D.J. asked.

Stephanie nodded. D.J. went to college nearby, and she was required to take one writing class. D.J. had signed up for a class called Writing for Children. Stephanie always thought it sounded like fun.

"Well, remember those Mary Mosley detective books we both liked when we were little?" D.J. went on. "The ones written by Grace Farrell?"

"Definitely!" Stephanie cried. "Those books are what made me want to be a writer in the first place!"

"I love those books too," Michelle put in.

"Well, guess what?" D.J. said. "Grace Farrell is coming to speak at my creative writing class next Thursday!"

"No way!" Stephanie cried. "That's so cool!"

"I know," D.J. said with a smile. "I bet she can teach me some great writing tricks!"

Stephanie laughed. "Like how to solve a mystery when the only clue is a shoelace that's put through the wrong hole?"

"Hey!" Michelle cried. "Don't tell me the end! I'm reading *Shoelace Secret* right now."

"I won't say a word," Stephanie promised.

"D.J., can I come see Grace Farrell with you?" Michelle asked. "She's my favorite writer of all time!"

"Yeah, that would be so cool," Stephanie said.

D.J. shook her head. "No way! Ms. Farrell is speaking in my class—she's sort of a guest teacher for the day. And I can't show up at class with my sisters!"

"Too bad," Stephanie said.

"Please?" Michelle cried.

D.J. laughed. "Michelle, come on," she said. "My professor would be mad if I just showed up with my little sister for no reason."

Comet came running into the room, his fluffy tail wagging furiously. He carried a tennis ball in his mouth.

"Oops! Sorry, Comet," Michelle said. "I forgot about you!" She grabbed her sneakers and hurried out of the room. Comet ran after her.

D.J. turned to Stephanie. "So what are you working on?"

Stephanie sighed. "I'm trying to write a note for Darcy," she said. "I mean, *from* Darcy."

"From Darcy?" D.J. asked. She perched on the white wicker chair next to Michelle's bed, and the light from the window made her short blond hair shimmer. "Why?"

"It's kind of cool," Stephanie replied. "We're reading *Cyrano* in English class, right?"

D.J. smiled. "I loved that play."

"Well," Stephanie explained, "Darcy likes this guy, Max. But she gets really shy around him and can't talk. So we figured she should write to him—like in *Cyrano*. That way Max can get to know the real Darcy."

"Sounds like a good idea," D.J. agreed.

"But since I'm a better writer than Darcy, *I'm* writing the note," Stephanie finished. "Only I'm kind of stuck for ideas."

D.J. frowned. "Now, that *doesn't* sound like a good idea," she commented. "How will Max get to know Darcy if you're the one writing the note? I mean, it's not exactly honest, is it?"

"I'm going to sound just like Darcy!" Stephanie insisted. "And I think it's pretty honest to help your best friend! What if Kimmy asked you to do something like this for her?"

Kimmy Gibler was D.J.'s best friend.

D.J. paused. "I guess I might do it," she said slowly. "But I think you're taking a big chance. If this guy—Max, right?—finds out, he could get really mad. And that wouldn't do Darcy any good at all. I just think it's a bad idea."

"Well, I think it's a great idea," Stephanie declared. "Max is never going to find out. Besides, Darcy needs my help. I have to do this for her!"

D.J. shrugged. "Hey, I'm just giving you my opinion," she said. "I don't want to see this backfire on you—or on Darcy."

Stephanie nodded. "I know," she replied. "But it will be fine. Really. It's going to work out great."

D.J. smiled. "You're probably right," she answered, getting to her feet. "I've got some stuff to work out too—my chemistry homework! See you later."

"See you," Stephanie echoed, watching her sister leave the room.

She glanced down at the sheet of paper in front of her again. *I'm supposed to be a good writer,* Stephanie thought. *But I can't come up with anything to say.*

Stephanie doodled on the paper, first drawing a girl wearing platform shoes, then a bouquet of flowers. She even drew a few hearts, hoping that would give her some ideas.

Inspiration, she thought. *That's what I need. I wonder where Cyrano got his inspiration?*

Stephanie snapped her fingers. *That's it!* she realized. She dug into her backpack and grabbed her copy of *Cyrano de Bergerac*. She flipped it open and began reading aloud.

" 'Oh, fair Roxane,' " she read.

"Oh, fair Max," she wrote.

No, that won't work, she told herself.

She read a few more lines from *Cyrano*. " 'Take my heart; I shall have it all the more; Plucking the flowers, we keep the plant in bloom.' "

It sounds great, but I don't even know what it means, Stephanie thought, slamming the book shut.

Stephanie thought for a moment more. "Your eyes are so brown, your hair is so blond," she wrote. But she couldn't think of anything to rhyme with blond.

"Your hair is so blond, your eyes are so brown, I think you're the cutest boy in town!"

Yuck! That is so geeky, Stephanie thought. *Darcy would never write that.*

Stephanie munched on another chocolate-chip-

54

nut cookie. *I can't do it*, she realized. *I just can't make myself sound like Darcy!*

But Darcy was counting on her, Stephanie knew. She had to write a love letter to Max!

Okay, Stephanie thought. *What would I say—if I totally liked Max?* She began to write:

Dear Max:

I really admire you and your plan to clean up Reese Park. It's awesome that you put that plan together. The neighborhood kids deserve a great place to play. I'll definitely be on hand for litter patrol on Wednesday. I have some other ideas for the cleanup too. I'd love to talk with you about them, but I'm a little shy. Can you figure out who I am? Here's a hint: I have a lot of goals!

Mystery Girl, Locker #122

Stephanie read the note over. *It's good*, she realized.

Now we'll see if it works.

CHAPTER
7

♦ ◀ ▸ ♦

"Aaaaaaaaah!" The piercing shriek carried down the school hallway as Stephanie and Allie stood at their lockers on Wednesday afternoon.

Allie was so startled that she dropped all of her books.

"What was *that?*" Stephanie asked.

"Steph! Allie!" the voice shrieked again. "You've got to come here! Now! You'll never believe it!"

"It's Darcy!" Allie cried.

Stephanie helped Allie scoop up her books. Then they both raced down the hall to Darcy's locker.

"Look at this!" Darcy screamed joyfully, waving a piece of paper in their faces.

Stephanie grabbed the paper and stared down at it.

"A note from Max!" she gasped. "It worked! My note worked! I mean, *Darcy's* note worked."

"You read it, Steph," Darcy begged, running her hands through her hair. "I can't. I'm too excited."

Stephanie read aloud:

"Dear Mystery Girl (Darcy Powell, ha ha—your locker number gave you away!),

"Thanks for the note. It was cool to get it. Thanks for the compliment too! I'd really like to hear your ideas for the cleanup. And by the way, what are your "goals" for the cleanup? (Sorry—I couldn't resist!) But seriously, tell me what you think we should do. Write back—you know the locker!

Mad Max

"P.S. Here's a joke: Why did the English teacher bring a pencil into his living room?

"To draw the curtains!

"(I'd tell you another joke about a pencil . . . but it doesn't have a point!)"

How corny! Stephanie thought. She felt a little disappointed. Max seemed so deep in person. But here he sounded so silly.

"Isn't this great?" Darcy gushed, clapping her hands in excitement. "It's so cute! He's so cute!"

"Totally cute," Allie agreed.

"But wait—Max wants to hear my ideas for the cleanup," Darcy said. "The only ideas I have are for field hockey defense!"

"What are you going to tell Max?" Allie asked.

Darcy shrugged. "I'm not sure." Then her face broke into a grin. "Stephanie, you have some ideas!" she said. "You have to write Max another note. Today! With plenty of suggestions for the cleanup!"

"But you're going to see Max later, remember?" Allie pointed out. "We're all supposed to go to Reese Park this afternoon and do litter patrol."

Darcy's grin faded quickly. "Oh, no! Is that today?" she asked. "I totally forgot—I thought it was tomorrow. Thursday is my only day without hockey practice. I have a really important practice this afternoon. We're putting some new moves into play."

"But, Darcy, I told Max in your note that you'd be coming to litter patrol! Don't you remember?" Stephanie said.

Darcy didn't answer.

Stephanie began to feel annoyed. "Darcy? You read the note, right?"

Darcy gave her a sheepish smile. "I meant to," she started. "But . . ."

"Darcy, I told you to read the note!" Stephanie cried. "Now Max will be expecting you to be at litter patrol! What's he going to think if you don't show up?"

"Oh, what should I do? What should I do?" Darcy moaned. She began pacing back and forth in front of her locker. "I'm dying to see Max, but I can't skip practice. I'm the captain—they *need* me!"

Suddenly she stopped pacing. "There's only one solution," she announced. "I'll come to Reese Park *after* practice."

"That might be too late," Stephanie warned her.

"I promise I'll be there!" Darcy said. "I'll run all the way. And I'll pick up twice as much litter as anyone else!"

"How does this look?" Stephanie asked after school. She and Allie were in the girls' bathroom, changing into their "litter patrol" clothes. Stephanie wore an oversized purple *Wake Up, San Francisco* T-shirt, old blue sweatpants, and a bright red baseball cap.

"Very . . . uh, litter-patrol chic!" Allie said with a giggle. "How about me?" she asked, twirling around in front of Stephanie.

"Fabulous!" Stephanie replied, laughing. Allie wore worn-out jeans that were ripped in a dozen places, and an old bleach-stained sweatshirt of her father's. It was so big that it hung down to her knees.

Allie frowned. "I wish Darcy were coming with us," she said.

"I know," Stephanie replied. "Max is definitely going to be wondering where she is. I just hope she doesn't get hung up in practice and miss the whole afternoon."

Allie and Stephanie hurried out of school. To save time, they caught the uptown bus to Reese Park instead of walking.

"Whew!" Stephanie exclaimed as they stepped off the bus near the park. "It really smells—even the air is dirty around here!"

"What a mess," Allie declared as they walked across the street and into the park.

Stephanie gazed around for a few seconds, amazed. Garbage covered most of the ground. The grass was overgrown with weeds. The pond in the middle of the park was entirely covered in green algae. Rusty, broken swings creaked in the breeze.

"It's even worse than in the pictures," Allie murmured. "How will we ever clean this up?"

"Well, it looks like we'll have plenty of help," Stephanie replied. She pointed to a spot on the banks of the pond, where about a dozen John Muir kids sat in a circle. Max, wearing a baggy black T-shirt and black jeans, sat in the middle.

"Let's go—we're late," Allie said.

As Stephanie followed Allie over to the circle, she heard Max giving instructions. "Okay, we need some people to start picking up the recyclable stuff—the paper, the bottles, and the cans," Max told the group. "That goes into the big gray bins by the sidewalk."

He held up a box of green plastic garbage bags and a basket full of thick cotton work gloves. "Everyone else can pick up the regular junk and stick it in these bags," he continued. "And everybody should take a pair of gloves to protect their hands."

Stephanie grabbed a plastic garbage bag and a pair of protective gloves. Then she and Allie began picking up the old, broken toys and rusty pieces of metal that littered the park ground.

Max and Paul were working nearby. Max moved quickly, scooping up handfuls of garbage and dropping it into his bag.

"Whew, it's really hot out here for the end of September," he commented.

Stephanie gestured toward the smelly green pond. "Why don't you go jump in the lake?" she suggested with a smile.

Max scowled at her. "Are you insulting *me?*" he asked. Then he grinned. "At least *I* don't have a big glob of Reese Park dirt on my nose!"

"I have dirt on my nose?" Stephanie cried in horror. She reached up to rub her nose—and a huge smear of mud came off.

"How embarrassing!" Stephanie laughed. "Well, I guess it's no surprise. One thing this park has plenty of is dirt."

Max chuckled. "Yeah," he replied. "And most of it is in the lake. If I jumped in there, I'd be smelling like Reese Park for days!"

Stephanie laughed.

"So how do you think this is working?" Max asked, stuffing garbage into his bag. "I mean, the cleanup?"

Stephanie gazed around at all the John Muir kids. "It's going pretty well . . ." she started.

"Is there a 'but' coming?" Max asked with a smile.

Stephanie nodded. "*But* we're spread out all over the place. Maybe we should focus on one part of the park—and get that cleaned up really well. That will make people feel like they've accomplished something."

"Great idea." Max nodded as he tied his garbage bag shut. "Then maybe some people can mow the grass and start planting bushes in that part of the park."

"Yeah!" Stephanie agreed. She picked up a tattered magazine from the ground. "And then we could take pictures of kids planting flowers, and send them to the local paper, and . . ."

"That will help us raise money!" Max finished her sentence.

Stephanie and Max smiled at each other. "I think you read my mind," Stephanie told him.

"You have great ideas," he said.

The sound of squealing brakes interrupted them. "Hey, the garbage truck is here," Max said, looking over Stephanie's shoulder. "Hold my place—I've got to make sure they pick everything up." He ran toward the street.

Max is a really great guy, Stephanie thought as she shoved the old magazine into her bag.

She glanced over at Allie—and frowned. Her best friend was staring at her with a strange look on her face.

"What's up?" Stephanie asked. "Why are you looking at me like I have three heads?"

Allie shrugged. "No reason," she replied. "But you and Max sure get along well."

"Yeah," Stephanie said, wiping her forehead. "I like him. He's cool. But *I'm* warm. Very warm." Her hair hung in damp strands in her face, and her arms felt as heavy as lead as she tossed another handful of garbage into the plastic bag. "And where is Darcy anyway? She should be here by now."

Allie shrugged.

A few minutes later Max ran back and picked up his garbage bag. "It's almost time to quit," he declared. "Can you guys spread the word? I'm going to dump this bag. Then I'm going to the deli to grab some sodas for everyone."

Stephanie nodded as Max dashed off.

"Hey, there's Darcy," Allie said.

Stephanie looked up from the garbage bag she was tying shut. Darcy walked slowly toward them, still wearing her hockey jersey and kilt. Her thick hair was damp with sweat, and her shoulders were slumped.

"It's about time," Stephanie told her. "We're almost finished."

Darcy plopped down on the ground. "Well, I'm definitely finished," she announced. "I'm wiped out. Practice was the worst. Everybody kept messing up."

"Darcy, I thought you were going to get here earlier," Stephanie complained.

Darcy sighed. "I tried, Steph, I really did," she said. "But everything kept going wrong. Jill Silber sprained her ankle and then Melissa Everett—she's our best goalie—told me that she won't be able to play in the big game. It's a tremendous mess."

"Hey, nice timing, Powell!" a voice called out.

Stephanie glanced up, hoping it was Max teasing Darcy. But it was his friend Paul, hauling two big bags of garbage past them. "We're just about done for the day," he added.

"Nice outfit," Darcy cracked back, suddenly smiling as she checked out Paul's wildly patterned Hawaiian shirt and his bright red sneakers.

"Well, I shop at the best store in town—my parents' basement!" he declared with a smile. "That's where I found the shirt anyway."

Darcy giggled. "I love that store," she replied. "All those awesome shirts from the seventies. Totally cool!"

"And Dad's old leisure suits," Paul joked. "They're amazing! Well, I've got to haul the rest of my garbage. See you later!"

"Sure. Later," Darcy said cheerfully as Paul walked away.

"Boy, you sure can talk around Paul," Stephanie declared. "If that were Max, you probably wouldn't have said one word!"

Darcy shrugged. "Paul is . . . I don't know, he's Paul," she replied. "He's easy to talk to. And he's just a friend, so I'm not nervous around him."

"I guess not," Stephanie replied. She checked her watch. "Listen, I have to get going. I promised Dad and Becky that I'd help chop the carrots and peppers for the salad—even if my arms do feel like they're ready to fall off!"

"I've got to go help with dinner too," Allie agreed.

Darcy frowned in disappointment. "But I haven't even seen Max," she complained.

Stephanie put her arm around Darcy's shoulders. "Don't worry, Darce," she said. "You'll see Max tomorrow—and everything will work out great."

But secretly Stephanie was beginning to think Max and Darcy didn't have anything in common. Maybe they never would get together, she thought.

Maybe they never *should* get together.

CHAPTER
8

◆ ◀ ◖ ◆

"We picked up so much garbage today, you wouldn't believe it!" Stephanie told her family that night over spaghetti and salad.

D.J. shook her head. "I *don't* believe it," she said. "How could Reese Park get so run-down in just a few years?"

"I guess it's been neglected," Danny replied. "It was a great park when you and Steph played there. But by the time Michelle was old enough to go there alone, I didn't want her to."

"Why?" Michelle asked. "I never knew Stephanie and D.J. got a park to play in and I didn't."

"The park had so much junk on the ground, we were afraid you would hurt yourself," Joey explained. "Plus, all the playground equipment

67

was falling apart. The city never repaired the broken swings or seesaws."

"It's a shame that Nicky and Alex won't be able to go to the park and play," Becky put in.

"But they will," Stephanie declared. "That park is going to be super-cool by the time we're done with it." She looked around the table at her family. "Will you guys help with the big cleanup? All the kids are asking their families."

"Sure," Becky replied, buttering a slice of bread. "We'll all help. Right?"

Everyone nodded.

"Max already has lots of other adults helping. He even called the city council to ask for money for park supplies," Stephanie continued. "And you should see all the kids he's got working! I mean, he's totally organized. And doing the work is fun because there are so many people involved." She dug happily into her spaghetti.

D.J. served herself some salad and grinned at Stephanie. "You're pretty excited about this, Steph," she teased. "What has you so enthusiastic? The cleanup? Or Max?"

"The cleanup, of course!" Stephanie exclaimed.

Jesse smiled. "Are you *sure*?" he asked.

Stephanie rolled her eyes. "Max is a great guy, and it's fun hanging out with him," she admitted. "But I joined the cleanup group only to help

Darcy out. And because it's a great cause. But mostly it's for Darcy. I mean, *she's* the one who likes Max!"

That is why I joined, right? Stephanie asked herself uncertainly. *Isn't that why I'm so excited?*

"Wait until you see this one!" Darcy exclaimed.

Stephanie and Allie had just walked into Darcy's bedroom on Saturday afternoon. Stephanie had spent the entire morning calling members of the San Francisco Parks Conservancy and asking them to give money for the Reese Park cleanup. She had gotten a few donations.

And now she was ready for fun.

Darcy waved a folded piece of paper in the air. "Max's latest letter!" she cried. "Who wants to read it?"

"Me, me!" Stephanie said, reaching for the note.

The three girls sank onto the yellow flowered rug. As Darcy and Allie dug into a bowl of pretzel nuggets, Stephanie unfolded the note. She began reading out loud.

"Dear Mystery Girl,
    "I think I'll keep calling you that, even though I know your name. It's kind of cute. Hey, we

missed you at litter patrol. It's too bad you had to stay so late at hockey practice. But I know you really have to stick with the team. Get it— stick? Hockey stick? Never mind! Anyway, your ideas in your last note were great—especially the one about having a party at the park for all the volunteers after the big cleanup. Meanwhile, I'm really egging everyone on to join in the cleanup. And that's no 'yolk!' Ha-ha. Am I funny or what?

"Mad Max"

"What an awesome note." Darcy sighed happily, leaning back against her yellow and white checked bedspread. "Max is so great in his notes. So funny."

Stephanie wrinkled her nose in distaste. "Funny?" she asked. "Those jokes are kind of lame, aren't they?"

"Well, I think he's funny," Darcy replied with a smile. "Thanks for writing him my excuse. It worked."

Stephanie nodded. She was glad to see Darcy so happy. But she was starting to feel a little weird about writing the notes. She couldn't help remembering what D.J. had said: "It's not really honest."

I do feel like I'm lying to Max, she thought. *Pretending my party idea is really Darcy's idea.*

Stephanie pushed those thoughts out of her head. "So, are we going blading today or what?" she asked.

"Definitely!" Darcy and Allie exclaimed.

"Well, let's go," Stephanie urged them.

When they reached Golden Gate Park, the three friends bladed down a long, winding path to Greenwood Field—a popular hangout for John Muir kids.

"Hey!" Allie exclaimed. "Look who's here!"

"Who?" Stephanie asked.

"Max!" Allie pointed. "Over there with that bunch of guys."

"Max?" Darcy cried, screeching to a stop.

Stephanie squinted at the field. About a dozen guys were spread out over the grass-and-dirt field, playing baseball. Max stood in the outfield. Stephanie made out his blond hair, baggy jean shorts, and light blue T-shirt.

"Look at him!" Darcy exclaimed. "He is so cute. So utterly, unbelievably adorable. I can't take it. I really can't."

"He is cute," Allie agreed.

"He's *really* cute," Stephanie said.

Allie shot her a curious look. Stephanie shrugged. "Well, he is," she said.

"Come on, let's go," Darcy urged. "I can't just stand here and stare at Max."

"But this is perfect!" Stephanie declared. "An excuse to hang out and watch Max play."

Darcy shook her head. "Let's just keep skating," she replied, doing a backward twirl. "I don't think we should bug Max while he's playing."

"Bug him?" Stephanie asked in amazement. "Max likes you. And you like him. Don't you want to be around him?"

Darcy skidded to a stop. "Of course I want to be around Max!" she cried. "I think about Max constantly! I just don't know what to say without you! I mean, I don't know if I'm ready to talk to him . . . yet."

"Darcy, you can't just keep writing him notes," Stephanie pointed out. "I mean, I can't just keep writing him notes."

Darcy did a quick figure eight on her blades. "I know," she said. "I just want to wait for the right time."

"Darcy, this is the right time," Stephanie insisted. "You don't have to have a major conversation. Just say hi when he comes in from the outfield."

"Or you could tell a joke," Allie suggested. "He keeps writing jokes in his notes to you."

Darcy shrugged.

"You don't have to be so nervous," Stephanie told her friend. "Just act normal—be Darcy Powell."

Darcy nodded. "I guess I know how to do that."

"Max's team is coming in," Allie said.

Darcy spun around on her skates. "Okay, okay. It's time for Operation Talk to Max. But you guys better be right behind me."

"We are!" Stephanie assured her.

The girls bladed to the edge of the field, where Max and his teammates were lined up waiting for their turns at bat. Max stood at the end of the line, talking to two other boys.

"Go up to him and say something," Allie urged. "Max doesn't even know you're here."

"Um, I will," Darcy replied. "Give me a minute."

Stephanie stared at her friend. Darcy wore a pinched, nervous expression on her face. *She's really afraid to talk to him*, Stephanie realized. *I have to help her.*

"Come on," she suggested. "Let's all go over to Max. We'll just ask him about the cleanup plans. It'll be easy."

Darcy smiled gratefully. "Good idea."

Stephanie led the way over to the end of the line. "Say something," she whispered to Darcy.

"No, you do it," Darcy whispered back. She looked pale and frightened. "Please."

Stephanie sighed. She tapped Max on the back. "Hi, Max," she said.

Max spun around. "Oh, hi!" he said with a big smile. "It's my cleanup crew!"

Stephanie laughed. "Yeah, but today we're clean—not covered with Reese Park dirt!"

Darcy hung back a little, standing right behind Stephanie. *She's just going to stand there*, Stephanie realized. *I have to make her say something.*

She took a step backward and elbowed Darcy, forcing her to step closer to Max. Now Darcy and Max stood face-to-face.

Stephanie and Allie stepped back.

"Um, want to hear a joke?" Darcy piped up.

"Sure," Max replied.

"What did one tonsil say to the other tonsil?"

Max shrugged. "You got me," he replied.

"Get dressed up. The doctor's coming," Darcy said. Then her face turned red. "Oh, that's not it," she said in a flustered voice. "Wait, give me a second. I'll remember the punch line."

Max stared at Darcy silently.

"The doctor's on his way?" Darcy tried. "No. I know! We better get dressed up—I hear the doctor's taking us out tonight. That's the right punch line! Oh, I ruined it!"

"That's okay, it doesn't sound funny anyway," Max replied.

Darcy's mouth dropped open.

"Um, I mean, it's okay," Max added quickly. "It-it's a very funny joke. . . ."

Max's voice trailed off. Stephanie thought he looked embarrassed.

Darcy scuffed at the grass with the toe of her left blade. Max jammed his hands into his shorts pockets.

"Um, so," Darcy murmured. "Um . . . how's the park cleanup going?"

"Oh, the cleanup? Oh, good," Max answered. "A carpenter in town might even build us some benches."

"Really?" Darcy murmured, staring at her feet. "Benches, huh?"

She's so nervous that she sounds bored, Stephanie thought. *This is awful!*

"Yeah, benches shaped like different animals and . . . things. . . ." Max frowned, realizing that Darcy didn't seem interested. "So, um, how's your team?" he asked. "Hockey, right?"

"Yeah, field hockey," Darcy replied. "Great, except these practices are taking—"

"Max, you're up!" a voice shouted.

"My turn at bat," Max explained. He shrugged. "Got to go. See you."

Darcy managed a weak smile. "Yeah, see you," she said. Max turned away from Darcy and ran up to the plate.

"Let's go," Darcy muttered to Stephanie and Allie. "Let's get out of here—fast." She pushed off hard on her skates, zooming away from the field.

"Uh-oh," Allie murmured. "She's really upset."

"We better catch up to her," Stephanie said.

They skated after her as fast as they could. After a few minutes, Darcy stopped and faced her friends.

"Well, that was a total disaster. Again," she exclaimed. "I don't get it. Max's notes are so funny. But in person he seems so different. Not funny at all."

"Well, not corny-funny anyway," Stephanie agreed. "In person, he seems more . . ."

"Quiet," Darcy finished for her. "I think that makes *me* quiet too. He's really hard to talk to!"

"He is not!" Stephanie cried. "I think Max is easier to talk to than most guys."

"Oh. Then maybe it's me," Darcy said. "He's so cute and I like him so much. I don't know what to do!" She sat on the ground and buried her face in her hands.

Stephanie and Allie exchanged glances.

"Maybe it's because Max is always distracted when you see him," Allie suggested.

"What do you mean?" Darcy asked, looking up.

"Well, he's either running a meeting or talking to somebody or playing baseball," she explained. "And then—surprise!—there you are. And neither of you knows what to say."

"Yeah!" Stephanie agreed. "Maybe you guys need to plan a time to get together. So you could figure out what to say and stuff. Like maybe . . . a date!"

Darcy was beginning to look interested.

"You could invite Max to your house for dinner," Allie suggested. "Your mom is such an excellent cook!"

"Maybe your mom could make her veggie lasagna," Stephanie added. "Yum! One bit of that and Max would love you for sure!"

Darcy giggled. "Steph!" she exclaimed. "How am I going to get to know Max better with my mom there?"

"You're right." Stephanie thought for a minute. "I know! Bowla Bowla!"

Bowla Bowla was an awesome new bowling

alley a few blocks from John Muir. It played the coolest music and the newest video games, and it even had roller-skating waitresses!

Stephanie had been there only once, when D.J. took her. But a group of John Muir ninth-graders—including Stephanie, Allie, and Darcy—were planning to go to Bowla Bowla in a few days.

"Bowla Bowla?" Darcy asked in confusion.

"Remember, we're all going on Wednesday," Stephanie reminded her. "Just invite Max to come too!"

Darcy bit her lip. "Will you ask him for me, Steph?" she asked. "You know, in one of your Cyrano notes?"

Stephanie sighed. "*Another* note?" she asked. "Darce, you know I'd do anything to help you with Max. But I don't think the notes are helping you and Max get to know each other better. And besides, this whole note thing is getting kind of icky. I thought I'd do it only once or twice. But now . . ."

Darcy stared at Stephanie with sad, pleading eyes. "But I really need your help," she begged. "If you won't ask him, I . . . I don't know what I'll do."

Stephanie groaned. "One more time," she told Darcy. "I mean it. This is the last note—ever."

CHAPTER
9

◆ ◀ ◆ ◆

Stephanie wrote in her notebook, sitting cross-legged on her bed that night.

Dear Mad Max,
Sorry I was so quiet at the park. I guess the cat got my tongue! Or something like that. Anyway, some of my friends are going to Bowla Bowla after school on Wednesday. I bet I can score more strikes than you. If you want to find out, come to Bowla Bowla too!
Mystery Girl

"What are you doing?" Michelle asked.
Stephanie looked up as Michelle dumped her backpack onto her bed.

"Writing another note for Darcy," Stephanie replied.

"Cool!" Michelle exclaimed. "Hey, can you do other handwriting as well as you can do Darcy's? Like Allie's or D.J.'s or Dad's?"

Stephanie shrugged. "Sure, it's easy," she replied. "Watch." On another piece of notebook paper, Stephanie carefully wrote "D. J. Tanner" with the same looping curlicues that D.J. always used. Then she wrote "Allie Taylor" in Allie's small, rounded handwriting.

"Wow! Do Dad's!" Michelle urged.

Stephanie slowly wrote "Danny Tanner" in Danny's plain, neat letters. Then she handed the paper to Michelle.

"Thanks!" Michelle exclaimed. "I'm going to practice these so I can do it too!" She folded the paper and stuffed it into the pocket of her jeans. Then she grabbed her book off the bed.

"Is that your Mary Mosley mystery?" Stephanie asked.

"Yeah—I have only three pages left to read," Michelle told her. "I want to finish it before Grace Farrell speaks at D.J.'s class. That way, if I have any questions about the mystery, D.J. can ask her to explain them."

Stephanie rolled her eyes. "I think Ms. Farrell

is going to talk about *writing*, not about mysteries," she said.

Michelle shrugged. "I'm going to go read in the living room. And then I'll practice these signatures!" she added, hurrying from the room.

Stephanie smiled and picked up her note to Max.

She had just finished rereading it, when the phone rang. She hurried out into the hallway and picked it up. "Hello?"

"Hi. Is this Stephanie?" a voice asked.

A guy's voice. A familiar voice.

"Yes. Who is this?" she asked.

"Oh, it's Max. Max Halsey," he replied. "You know, from the park cleanup?"

"Right, Max from the cleanup," Stephanie said calmly. But she didn't *feel* calm. She felt happy and excited, and her heart began beating fast.

"I wanted to let you know that your phone calls—to those people in the Parks Conservancy—really helped," Max declared. "Bigtime."

"Really? What do you mean?" Stephanie asked. "Did someone donate money?"

"Even better," Max replied. "Someone is donating playground equipment—a swing set and a couple of seesaws. Brand new!"

"Max, that's excellent," Stephanie cried. *Why*

am I so totally happy to be talking to him on the phone? she wondered. *Is it just because of the playground?*

"Pretty great," he agreed. "Since it was your phone call that got the equipment, do you want to come on Monday when my uncle Tim and I pick the stuff up?"

"Um . . . I'm not sure if I can," Stephanie said. "Maybe you should ask someone else to go."

Like Darcy, she added silently.

"Well, I asked Darcy. But she's got hockey practice, of course."

"Of course," Stephanie repeated. But she couldn't believe her ears. Max had asked Darcy to spend time with him? And she had said *no? How could she do that?* Stephanie wondered.

"Stephanie? You still there?" Max asked.

"Oh! Yeah," she stammered. "Sorry—I was just, um, looking at my calendar. Monday, you said? I guess I could go with you. It would be fun to see the swings and seesaw."

And fun to spend the time with you, she couldn't help thinking.

"Okay, we'll stop by your house Monday after school," Max said. "And, hey, thanks for introducing me to Darcy—her idea to call the Parks Conservancy was terrific. I mean, between her idea and your phone call, we got a whole new playground!"

"Uh, yeah. Great," Stephanie said. "Well, see you Monday."

Stephanie hung up the phone, all her excitement gone. *I wish he'd called to tell me how great my idea was*, Stephanie thought. *But he thinks that idea was* Darcy's. *He thinks everything I say about the park comes from* Darcy.

She stared at the note in her lap. Because of these notes, Max wasn't getting to know the real Darcy.

Even worse, he wasn't getting to know the real Stephanie.

And I sure wish he would, Stephanie admitted to herself.

"Guess what?" Darcy cried as she slid into her seat in the lunchroom on Monday. "I got a reply from Max! And we just gave him the new note this morning! Here, I'll read it."

"Dear Mystery Girl,
"I told you I was going to keep calling you that. Sorry you can't come with me to get the swing set today. But Bowla Bowla sounds totally cool. I'll meet you there on Wednesday at four.

And get ready for some serious competition—they don't call me Strike for nothing!

Mad Max

"P.S. Did you hear about the car with the wooden engine and the wooden wheels? It wooden go! Get it—'wooden'?"

"Can you believe it?" she squealed happily, unwrapping her tuna fish sandwich. "We're going on a date! A date! Well, sort of a date. What am I going to say? What am I going to wear?"

"Wear your black and white polka dot minidress," Allie suggested. "That will look so cute with bowling shoes."

Darcy frowned. "Is that too dressy?" she asked. "I was thinking jeans and a T-shirt. Max is pretty casual."

"How about your yellow jeans?" Stephanie suggested, lifting her egg salad sandwich to her mouth.

"Perfect!" Darcy cried. "Now I just have to figure out what to say to him." She smiled at Stephanie. "Maybe I should send *you* in my place—you don't have any trouble talking to Max."

"She could wear a Darcy mask," Allie joked, grabbing a celery stick from her lunch tray.

"Or stand behind me and tell me what to say—just like Cyrano with Christian," Darcy added with a giggle.

"Very funny," Stephanie replied. But she didn't really think it was funny. In fact, she felt sort of guilty. *I should tell Darcy I'm going to pick up that playground equipment with Max today,* she thought. *But I don't want to.*

I wish I could tell Max that I'm the one writing the notes, she thought. *But I can't. Darcy likes Max and I promised to help her.*

She heard Darcy and Allie talking, but she wasn't really listening to them. She took a bite of her sandwich and imagined herself confessing to Max. She imagined Max smiling back at her and saying, "I'm so glad it was really you."

Stephanie shook herself out of her daydream. *This is awful,* she thought with a sinking feeling. *I can't do this to Darcy.*

I can't like Max.

But Stephanie knew it was too late. She already *did* like Max.

A lot.

"Hi, Steph," Michelle cried as Stephanie rushed into their bedroom that afternoon. Michelle was sitting on the rug, writing in a note-book. "Guess what I'm doing?"

"Huh?" Stephanie asked as she dashed to her closet and began digging through her sweaters. She was looking for her blue cropped sweater, the one that matched her eyes.

"Signatures," Michelle announced proudly. "Want to see?"

"What?" Stephanie asked. *Where is that sweater?* she wondered. *It's perfect for my non-date with Max!* She gave up on the closet and began searching through a dresser drawer.

"Do you want to see my signatures?" Michelle asked again, holding up the notebook. "They're pretty good."

"Hmm? Oh, sure!" Stephanie said, finally hearing her sister. She took the notebook from Michelle's hands. "These are good! But you need to do the Ds loopier on D.J.'s signature. And I can tell that you picked up the pen a lot—you know, stopped and started again. It's better to write the words all at once."

"Okay, loopier Ds and hold down the pen," Michelle repeated. "Thanks, Steph."

Just then, a horn beeped outside. Max!

"Got to go," Stephanie told Michelle, giving up on the blue sweater. She threw a red jacket over her school clothes. "Bye!"

Stephanie ran downstairs and yanked open the door. Max stepped out of the passenger seat of a large silver truck. "Climb aboard!" he called out with a smile.

Stephanie dashed toward the truck and slid in between Max and his uncle. *I'm sitting next to Max*, she thought with a shiver. It felt strange. But nice.

"Stephanie, this is my uncle Tim," Max said.

Uncle Tim tipped his baseball cap at Stephanie. "Your partner in *grime*, Max?" he joked as he pulled away from the curb.

Stephanie and Max laughed. *Maybe that's where Max learned those corny jokes he uses in his notes*, she thought. Uncle Tim kept telling jokes and stories all the way to the house where they picked up the playground equipment.

As they drove away from the house, Max flipped on the radio. *The Rush Hour Renegades* blasted from the speakers.

"Cool!" Max declared. "I love these guys."

"Really?" Stephanie asked. "Jesse's my uncle," she said proudly. "And Joey Gladstone is my dad's best friend. They live with us."

Max's jaw dropped in surprise. "No joke?" he asked. "I listen to them every day!"

"No joke," Stephanie answered, smiling at Max. "I listen to them constantly. I have to—

they're always trying out their new routines at home!"

"That is totally cool!" Max exclaimed. "Are you into the music they play?"

Stephanie nodded. "Definitely," she replied. "I love all that disco from the seventies."

"Me too!" Max proclaimed. "See, Uncle Tim, she's not just a great park-cleaner, she's also got awesome taste in music."

Uncle Tim winked at Stephanie.

She felt her cheeks get warm. "Jesse even made me these amazing tapes," she told Max. "All the best dance songs from the past twenty years."

"I'd love to hear them sometime," Max replied. He snapped his fingers. "Hey! You know the party we're going to have after the big cleanup? The one Darcy thought up?"

You mean the party I thought up, Stephanie wanted to say. But she just nodded. "Sure—the party in Reese Park."

"We want to have dancing—your tapes would be perfect," Max said. "Would you bring them?"

"To the party? Definitely," Stephanie replied.

"That would be great," Max said. "Boy, I'm dying of thirst. Want to stop at my house for something to drink?"

"Sure," Stephanie said.

"Is that okay, Uncle Tim?" Max asked.

"No problem," he answered. After a few more blocks, Uncle Tim pulled up in front of a neat white house. Stephanie and Max jumped from the truck. Uncle Tim followed.

"Come on in," Max said. He opened the door and waved Stephanie inside. A woman with short blond hair, wearing jeans and a T-shirt, greeted them in the living room.

"Hi, honey," she said to Max. "Hi, Tim." She gave Stephanie a friendly smile. "And who is this?" she asked.

"Mom, this is my friend Stephanie," Max replied. "She's been helping with the cleanup."

My *friend* Stephanie. The words hit Stephanie like a slap in the face.

That's all I am to Max, she thought. *A friend. Darcy is the one he wants for a girlfriend.*

"Nice to meet you, Stephanie," Ms. Halsey said. "How about some lemonade?"

"Sounds good. Thanks," Stephanie answered.

Max's mother started into the kitchen. "Oh, Max, a Mr. Buyers called for you," she said over her shoulder. "The phone number is on the counter."

"Mr. Buyers?" Max repeated, his brown eyes lighting up in excitement.

He turned to Stephanie. "Mr. Buyers is on the city council," he explained. "I've got to call him—maybe they're going to give us the Dumpster and the plants that I asked for!"

Stephanie followed Max into the red and white kitchen and sat down at the table. Max grabbed the phone and dialed quickly.

"Hi, Mr. Buyers? This is Max Halsey. You know, from the Reese Park cleanup."

Stephanie couldn't help smiling as she watched him. Max seemed so sure of himself, even talking to a city council member. *This cleanup is really important to him,* she thought.

Suddenly a deep frown crossed Max's face. "But . . . but I thought . . ." he stammered. "Okay. Good-bye."

Max slammed the phone back into its cradle. "I can't believe this!" he cried.

"What's wrong?" Stephanie asked in alarm. "Aren't we getting the Dumpster and plants?"

"We're not getting anything!" Max replied, scowling. "The city is going to sell the Reese Park land!"

"*Sell* it?" Stephanie gasped. "Why?"

"He said the park is too expensive to keep up," Max explained. "Even if we clean it up, the city can't afford to *keep* it clean. But they can get a lot of money for the land—and use it for other city programs."

"But that's not fair!" Stephanie exclaimed. "We already have this playground equipment. And the kids in that neighborhood deserve to have Reese Park! Kids like my cousins Nicky and Alex—they need a place to play."

"Right," Max agreed, pacing the floor. "We can't let the city council take Reese Park away. We have to take action!"

"How about a petition?" Stephanie suggested. "We'll get everybody at school to sign it. Then we'll bring it to the council—to show them how much people want to keep Reese Park."

"Yeah!" Max exclaimed. "But instead of just bringing the *petition* to the council, we should bring them the *people!*"

Stephanie thought for a moment. "You mean like a demonstration?" she asked. "That's perfect. Great idea!"

Max nodded. "There's a council meeting on Thursday," he said. "We can have a demonstration there. Come on, we have plans to make!"

Max grabbed a pad of paper and two pens from the kitchen counter. Then he sat down next to Stephanie and handed her a sheet of paper and a pen.

"Okay," Max said. "First we'll call everyone

who volunteered for the cleanup and ask them to be there."

"Check," Stephanie replied. "I'll get people to make posters and flyers to hand out at neighborhood stores."

"Great," Max agreed. "Paul and some of the other guys can get in touch with people around town and ask them to go to the demonstration too."

Boy, Stephanie thought as she and Max formed their plan. *Max and I really make a great team! I bet we'd make a great couple too.*

CHAPTER
10

◆ ◀ ▶ ◆

"Allie, it's me," Stephanie said when her friend picked up the phone. She had tried to call Darcy the minute she got home from Max's house, but Darcy's line was busy.

"What's up, Steph?" Allie asked.

"We've got a problem," Stephanie told her. "The city wants to sell Reese Park. We're going to have a demonstration on Thursday. Will you help me make flyers?"

"Of course," Allie replied.

"Okay, I have to go," Stephanie said. "I'll call you later!"

She dialed Darcy's number again. Busy.

Stephanie waited a few minutes, then called Darcy again. This time it rang. "Darce? It's

Steph," she said quickly. "Your line was busy for about half an hour!"

"I know," Darcy replied. "I was talking hockey strategy with Paul. He has some great ideas for—"

Stephanie cut her off. "This is no time for hockey," she told her friend. Then she repeated what she told Allie. "Will you make signs for the demonstration?"

"Definitely," Darcy exclaimed. "Maybe I can get the whole team to pitch in. How did you hear about this?"

"Uh, Max told me," Stephanie replied, trying to sound casual. "I went with him and his uncle to pick up some playground equipment."

Stephanie felt a little guilty, remembering how much fun she'd had with Max. *I don't want Darcy to think I'm trying to steal him away from her*, she thought.

Even if I do like Max more than I should.

"The playground equipment, right," Darcy answered. "Max asked me to go—but I had practice. Did he say anything about me? I mean, Wednesday is our Bowla Bowla date." She giggled.

"He was kind of distracted by the bad news about the park," Stephanie pointed out. "But I'm sure Max is looking forward to your date too," she added quickly.

"I'm going to have so much fun with him," Darcy exclaimed.

Lucky you, Stephanie thought sadly.

"Think she'll be late again?" Allie joked.

It was Wednesday afternoon, and Stephanie and Allie stood outside the front door of the school. They were waiting for Darcy to finish practice so they could walk over to Bowla Bowla.

"No way," Stephanie said. "Darcy can't wait to get to her date with Max. I think she'll finally be able to really talk to him today."

"There you are!" Darcy cried, bursting through the door. Stephanie was surprised to see that her friend still wore a hockey uniform.

"Darcy, what's with the outfit?" Stephanie asked. "You're not wearing that to Bowla Bowla, are you?"

"No," Darcy moaned. She paced back and forth nervously. "It's horrible. Just horrible. I thought it was going to be a short practice. But Coach says we have to spend another hour. I'm the captain—I can't leave now! I just can't!"

"But, Darcy, we're supposed to be at Bowla Bowla at four o'clock," Stephanie declared. "That's in ten minutes!"

"Steph, you've got to tell Max I'm going to be late," Darcy begged. "I'll run to Bowla Bowla the second practice is over. I promise! Tell him I'll be there as soon as I can."

"Darcy, every chance you have to see Max gets messed up by hockey practice," Stephanie pointed out.

"Don't you think I know that?" Darcy exclaimed. "But what am I supposed to do, let the team down?"

"No, of course not," Stephanie replied. "But what am I supposed to say to Max?"

"Tell him I had a hockey emergency," Darcy begged. "Please! I have to go—the coach is waiting." Darcy turned and dashed back toward the field.

Stephanie threw her hands up in the air. "Great! This is just great!" she cried.

Allie stared at Stephanie, her green eyes wide with surprise. "Darcy's the one who's going to miss out on spending time with Max," she pointed out. "So how come *you're* upset?"

"I'm not upset," Stephanie protested. "It's just that I've been helping Darcy—a lot. I mean, writing those notes and making excuses for her with Max . . ."

Allie raised an eyebrow. "Are you sure there's not something else bugging you?"

Stephanie stared at her friend's calm, kind face. She really wanted to tell Allie about her secret feelings for Max. In fact, she felt as if the truth would burst out of her if she didn't tell someone.

"There *is* something else bugging me," she admitted. "But it's horrible. Really horrible."

Allie looked at Stephanie with concern. "What's going on?" she asked.

"*Max* is what's going on," Stephanie said slowly. "I've been spending a lot of time with him—planning the cleanup and all. And he's great—he's just a really great guy. And now—"

Stephanie stopped talking. How could she admit that she liked Darcy's guy?

"Now what?" Allie asked gently.

"I like him," Stephanie admitted. "I mean, I *really* like him."

Allie's eyes opened wide. "You do?" she asked. "But . . . wow. What are you going to do?"

Stephanie shrugged. "What *can* I do?" she asked unhappily. "Darcy likes Max and he likes her—even though they can barely talk to each other in person."

"Wow," Allie said again. "This is really bad."

Stephanie stared at her anxiously. "Please don't tell Darcy that I like Max, Allie," she pleaded. "I don't want her to think I'm trying to steal him from her or anything."

"I won't say a word," Allie promised. "Now, come on, let's go bowling," she added gently. "Max will be waiting."

Yeah, Stephanie thought. *Waiting for Darcy.*

The neon Bowla Bowla sign glowed brightly in the afternoon sun. It showed a large green bowling ball with hot-pink pins.

As Stephanie and Allie entered Bowla Bowla, Madonna's latest song blasted from the sound system. Hundreds of tiny colored lights glittered on the ceiling. Waitresses wearing pink leggings and oversized black and pink striped T-shirts skated around the wooden floor, carrying trays of burgers and shakes and fries.

Kids from John Muir were gathered in small groups at the end of almost every lane.

This will be fun, Stephanie thought, feeling her mood lift.

"There's Max," Allie said, pointing to a lane at the far end of the bowling alley. "He's with Paul."

Stephanie spotted Max's blond hair. She was glad to see him smiling as he joked with Paul and some other guys. Max had been so serious ever since he found out about the city council selling Reese Park.

But he's probably excited about his date with Darcy today, she realized. *That's why he looks happy.*

Stephanie and Allie rented their bowling shoes and made their way to Max's lane. "Hey, it's my Reese Park demonstration committee," Max said, grinning at Stephanie. Then a puzzled look crossed his face. "Where's Darcy?" he asked.

"She'll be here, but she'll be kind of late," Stephanie replied. "She had a . . . um, a hockey emergency."

"A hockey *emergency?*" Max asked. He frowned. "Well, I hope she gets here soon. I can't wait too long—I have a lot to do for the demonstration."

"I know," Stephanie said sympathetically.

Max shrugged. "Let's bowl," he declared. "I guess Darcy can join the game when she gets here."

"All right!" Paul exclaimed. "Boys against girls! Me first!" He grabbed a gray and white bowling ball from the bin. "Too light," he said. He tried a blue one next. "Too heavy."

Finally, he picked up a bright purple and green ball with wild orange lines zigzagging all over it. "Too ugly!" he declared with a grimace.

Stephanie and Allie laughed.

Max shook his head. "Paul, are we going to be here all day waiting for you to pick a ball?" he teased.

"A master bowler must have the perfect ball," Paul replied with a grin. He grabbed a plain black ball and stood at the top of the lane. Then he pulled his arm back—and bowled a strike.

"Beat *that!*" he teased Max.

Max yanked a ball from the bin. "Now watch the *real* master bowler at work," he told Allie and Stephanie. He pulled his arm back—and hurled the ball into the aisle.

Plonk! It fell right into the gutter.

Stephanie burst out laughing.

"That was just my warmup," Max joked.

"Right," Paul answered. He grinned at Stephanie and Allie. "They don't call him the gutterball king for nothing."

"My turn!" Stephanie cried. She picked up a pink ball and threw it into the lane. It plopped into the gutter.

"Whoops," she said with a giggle. "That was just my warmup."

"Hey," Max protested. "That's *my* excuse!"

"And it's a great one," Stephanie answered with a laugh.

Stephanie plopped down on the bench as Allie took her turn—and bowled a strike.

"Any more progress on demonstration stuff?" Max asked, sitting next to Stephanie.

"Definitely," Stephanie answered. "My whole family is going to help out. In fact, Joey and Jesse are announcing it this afternoon on *The Rush Hour Renegades!*"

"That's excellent!" Max exclaimed. "Did you hear that, Paul? Great work, Steph. I knew I could count on you."

"Well, I'm glad you're happy about something," Paul teased him. "Because it's your turn to bowl again—and that will be depressing!"

Max picked up his ball. "Thanks to Stephanie's news, I'm ready for anything," he announced.

"Soda break!" Paul proclaimed at about five-fifteen. Everyone had bowled three games.

"It's almost go-home-for-dinner break for me," Stephanie whispered to Allie. "I've got to leave soon."

"Me too," Allie answered. "And Darcy's not even here yet."

"Poor Max," Stephanie murmured. "Darcy is always standing him up."

"Let's just hope that when she gets here, she doesn't start hiccuping again," Allie joked.

"About time, Powell!" Paul called.

Stephanie looked up to see Darcy racing

toward them. "What an awesome practice," she cried happily, her black hair bouncing as she ran. "We're definitely going to win—we're definitely going to beat Cliffside. I am totally happy!"

"Darcy, how do you really feel?" Paul asked. "Come on, don't be so shy."

Stephanie smiled as Paul teased her friend. Darcy was the least-shy person she knew. When Darcy was happy, everybody heard about it.

Darcy stuck her tongue out at Paul. "Very funny," she replied, her face still flushed with excitement. "You'd be pretty happy too if your team had such an excellent practice!"

"What happened at practice?" Paul asked seriously. He leaned forward in his chair to talk to Darcy.

"It wasn't anything big, really," Darcy explained. "We just moved a couple of players around, like you and I talked about the other day."

Paul nodded.

"And what a difference!" Darcy cried. "We were totally clicking—scoring like crazy!"

"Sounds wild!" Paul exclaimed. "Hey, want to take over the soccer team too? I think we could use you!"

Darcy grinned. "Sorry—you guys are on your

own," she replied. "But I might lend you my shin guards!"

Paul and Darcy burst into laughter.

Stephanie, finishing up her soda, saw that Max was watching Darcy. But Darcy was so busy telling Paul about her practice that she didn't even notice.

Max checked his watch. *I guess he has to leave soon too*, Stephanie thought.

"We should try to get Darcy to notice him," Allie whispered.

Stephanie sighed. She didn't really want Max to notice Darcy—she wanted Max to notice *her*. She wanted him to realize that she was the girl who had been writing to him all along. She was the girl who gave him ideas for the park cleanup.

But Darcy is my best friend, Stephanie reminded herself. *She likes Max, and Max likes her. I have to help her.*

"Max," Stephanie said in a loud voice. "Is there anything else that needs to be done for tomorrow? You know, for the demonstration?"

Max nodded. "Paul's going to help me finish my speech—for the council," he replied. "And I have to make sure that the little kids who live near Reese Park are all set to come."

"I can call their moms if you need me to,"

Stephanie volunteered. "And of course Darcy's making most of the signs—right, Darcy?"

"And then the goalie . . ." Darcy was explaining to Paul.

"Uh, Darcy?" Stephanie repeated.

"What?" Darcy asked, breaking off in midsentence.

Stephanie gave her a talk-to-Max look.

Darcy's eyes flew open wide. "Oh, sorry!" she cried. "I guess I was so psyched about the practice that I was rambling on to Paul."

Or you were afraid to talk to Max, Stephanie thought.

Darcy gave Max an embarrassed little wave. He waved back.

"You'll have your signs ready for tomorrow, right?" Stephanie asked her.

"Signs?" Darcy looked puzzled for a second. "Oh, right—for the demonstration. I'm going to make them tonight," she said.

Stephanie frowned. "You mean you haven't started making them yet? But we need so many. Are you sure you'll have time?"

"Of course," Darcy said. "I'm devoting the whole night to sign making."

"Promise?" Stephanie asked.

Darcy laughed. "Yes, worrywart, I promise," she said. "These signs will be the coolest demonstration posters in history. Plus, I'm going to bring the whole hockey team to the demonstration with me. And believe me, they're loud!"

"Loud? That's great," Max replied. He checked his watch again. "Well, I've got to go." He gave Darcy a shy grin. "Can I walk you home?" he asked.

Darcy nodded, looking down at her feet. "Sure," she replied. "That would be really nice."

"Okay," Max said quietly. "And you can tell me all about your hockey team. Like, when is your next game?"

"We call them matches, not games," Darcy explained.

"Oh, right," Max replied uneasily. "That's interesting."

Stephanie watched Max and Darcy walk away together, still talking.

I should feel great, she thought. *Finally, Darcy and Max are together—at least for a walk home.*

So why do I feel so lousy?

Stephanie couldn't help answering her own question: *Because I wish that Darcy didn't like Max.*

And I wish Max liked me.

CHAPTER
11

◆ ◥ ◣ ◆

"Does somebody want to explain this?" D.J. demanded.

Stephanie glanced up from her math homework. D.J. stood in the door of the bedroom, waving a piece of loose-leaf paper.

"What's that?" Michelle asked from her bed. She lay on her stomach, reading another mystery book.

"This is a note from Dad saying that I have to take you to college with me tomorrow afternoon, Michelle," D.J. announced.

"Why?" Stephanie asked.

"Because Dad has to work late," Michelle said quickly. "And everyone else is going to be with you at the demonstration, Stephanie. He doesn't want me to be at home alone."

Stephanie gasped. "Dad's not coming to my Reese Park demonstration?" she cried. "But I need everyone to be there!"

Michelle's face turned red. "Well, um . . . he must be going to the demonstration straight from the TV station," she said. "So he wants D.J. to watch me."

"But, Michelle, I have classes tomorrow afternoon," D.J. said. "And you could go to the demonstration with Stephanie and the rest of the family."

Michelle opened her mouth to speak, but no words came out. Her face got even redder.

Stephanie watched her, confused. "Yeah, Michelle," she said. "It seems weird that Dad would want you to tag along to D.J.'s classes."

"That's not the only weird thing," D.J. put in. "Take a look at this note from Dad." She handed the paper to Stephanie.

Stephanie studied the note. It was written in pencil, and the words slanted backward. Some of them were written in big letters, and some were written in small letters. And "demonstration" was spelled wrong.

Stephanie burst out laughing. "Dad didn't write this!" she cried.

"Exactly," D.J. agreed. "Do you want to explain, Michelle?"

Michelle looked down at her hands. "I didn't think you could tell that it wasn't Dad's handwriting. I practiced it, just like Stephanie showed me."

Stephanie stopped laughing. "Michelle!" she cried. "What do you mean, like *I* showed you? I never told you to forge a note from Dad!"

"You taught me how to write in Dad's handwriting," Michelle said. "And I just really wanted to see Grace Farrell at D.J.'s class tomorrow."

Stephanie and D.J. exchanged glances.

"Oh, so that's what this is all about," D.J. said. She plopped down on the end of Michelle's bed. "Michelle, I can't take you to class with me. Try to understand—you would be bored, and it would distract the other students in my class."

Michelle nodded sadly.

"And anyway," Stephanie put in, "you should be punished for forging a note from Dad. That's just . . . just wrong! It's like lying."

Michelle frowned in confusion. "But you wrote notes in Darcy's writing," she protested. "And that wasn't wrong, was it?"

"Michelle, that's different," Stephanie declared. "Darcy *asked* me to write the notes."

Michelle still looked confused.

"Darcy *wanted* me to pretend I was her,"

Stephanie explained. "And I did it for Darcy. But Dad didn't ask you to pretend you were him— you did it only to get something *you* wanted. There's a big difference. Get it?"

"I guess," Michelle mumbled. She looked up at Stephanie and D.J. "You guys won't tell Dad, will you?" she asked. "Please don't tell!"

"We won't tell," D.J. said.

"We won't tell as long as you never forge Dad's name again," Stephanie said.

"I won't," Michelle said. "I promise."

"Good. And I'll tell you all about Grace Farrell," D.J. said, getting to her feet. "See you guys later."

When D.J. was gone, Michelle let out a sigh. "I guess I'm not as good at copying handwriting as you are."

Stephanie shrugged. "I'm beginning to think it's not such a great thing to learn," she admitted. "I know Darcy asked me to write the notes. But it turned out to be kind of a bad idea."

"How come?" Michelle asked.

"Well, Max likes Darcy—because he thinks Darcy wrote the notes. Only she didn't. And *I* like Max, but he doesn't know how much I like him," Stephanie explained. "It's a real mess."

"Wow," Michelle agreed. "It sure sounds like a mess. What are you going to do?"

Stephanie sighed. "I'm not sure. I guess I have to try to stop liking Max."

"Can you do that?" Michelle asked.

"I don't know," Stephanie said. "But I'll find out tomorrow."

"There must be a hundred people here!" Stephanie exclaimed to Allie. She glanced nervously around the crowd outside the city council building.

It was Thursday afternoon, and the demonstration was supposed to start in half an hour. People were gathered on the cement patio outside the white marble building, chattering and laughing.

Max's uncle Tim had parked his pickup truck off to one side of the crowd. He was setting up a recycling demonstration. Jesse and Joey had a booth on the other side of the crowd, and were broadcasting live over the radio. Stephanie, Allie, Danny, Becky, and Michelle were gathered around the booth.

"Allie, do you see Darcy?" Stephanie asked, standing on tiptoe to look over the crowd. "She's supposed to be here with the signs she made."

Allie shook her head. "No sign of Darcy yet," she replied.

Stephanie spotted Max making his way

through the crowd toward her. He was all dressed up—in khakis and a white shirt. He even wore a tie!

"Steph, I think it's time to start passing out the signs," Max declared. "I hope we have enough for everybody."

"Okay, the kids from the French Club have signs to give out. And Bonnie Howard and her friends are already waving their signs. But, uh, Darcy's not exactly . . . um, here yet with hers," Stephanie admitted. "I'm sure she's on her way."

"All right," Max said nervously. "I'll start passing out the ones we have. Let me know when Darcy shows up."

Max hurried away.

"Steph! Allie!" a voice called through the crowd. "Where are you?"

Darcy!

"Over here! By the radio booth!" Stephanie cried, jumping up and down and waving her arms to attract Darcy's attention.

Darcy elbowed her way through the crowd. "Sorry I'm so late," she gasped when she reached the booth. "I was talking to my coach after school, and I didn't realize what time it was."

"Do you have the signs?" Stephanie asked. "We have to give them out right away."

111

Darcy's mouth dropped open. "Coach called me last night," she said. "We were on the phone for like two hours. And then she asked me to meet with her today, and—"

"The signs," Stephanie interrupted. She was starting to get a bad feeling. A really bad feeling. "Where are they?"

Darcy cringed. "I meant to do them," she said, chewing her bottom lip. "I even got the posterboard. But I just couldn't get it together."

"Are you telling me you didn't make them?" Stephanie demanded. "You didn't make *any*?"

"I'm really sorry," Darcy declared, holding her hands out pleadingly. "I couldn't help it. The team . . ."

"Darcy, you promised to make signs!" Stephanie said angrily. "You *promised!*"

Allie stared at both of them, wide-eyed.

"But, Steph," Darcy started. "I . . ."

"Oh, forget it!" Stephanie cried. She turned and stomped away, leaving Darcy calling after her. "Steph, please don't be mad. What can I do?"

Stephanie pushed her way through the crowd until she spotted Max standing near the steps to the council building. He was surrounded by a group of little kids who lived near Reese Park.

"Max!" Stephanie cried. "We have a problem."

Max turned to her. "What's going on?" he asked.

"The signs," Stephanie panted. "Darcy didn't make them. Now we won't have enough for everybody."

Max blinked. "Okay," he said slowly. "We have ten minutes before the council gets here. We need a plan. A *quick* one."

Stephanie looked around. People, people, and more people.

Then her eyes fell on Uncle Tim's truck. In order to show the council how the cleanup crew was recycling, he had filled the back of the pickup truck with plastic bins. The bins overflowed with used bottles and cans, neat stacks of old newspapers, and piles of flattened cardboard boxes tied up with string.

Stephanie smiled. She had the perfect solution.

"The boxes," she told Max. "We can make signs from the cardboard boxes in Uncle Tim's truck."

Max nodded, slowly at first, then faster. "Yeah, that'll work," he declared. "Come on," he cried to the neighborhood kids.

"I'll get some pens and markers," Stephanie offered.

Max herded the kids toward Uncle Tim's truck. Stephanie ran through the crowd, borrowing pens from everyone she could find. Then she made her way to the pickup.

Max climbed onto the bed of the truck and then turned to help Stephanie up. From there she could see the whole crowd—including her family standing with Allie and Darcy at the *Rush Hour Renegades* booth.

Darcy looks upset, Stephanie noticed. *Maybe I was too hard on her about the signs. I'll apologize after the demonstration.*

"We'd better work fast," Max told her as he untied a stack of boxes. Max and Stephanie unflattened the boxes. Then they tore the sides and tops off to use as signs.

"What should we write?" Max asked, holding a black felt pen.

"How about 'We Want Park!'" Stephanie suggested.

"Excellent!" Max said. "Or, 'Park It at Reese Park!'"

Stephanie giggled. "Whatever that means. Or . . . 'Leave Reese Park Perky.'"

Max chuckled. "A perky park?" he asked with a smile. "Exactly *what* is a perky park?"

Stephanie laughed as she lettered another sign. "Beats me," she admitted. "But it might get some attention. Now we'd better start giving these out."

Max nodded. He began handing signs to the neighborhood kids who stood below them. "Pass these out," he told them. "Fast! Then come back for more."

Stephanie and Max kept lettering. Finally, everyone in the crowd—including all the kids—was holding up signs that read: WE WANT OUR PARK! DON'T SELL REESE PARK! and other slogans.

With the last two pieces of cardboard, Stephanie and Max wrote signs for themselves.

Stephanie's read: LEAVE REESE IN PEACE.

Max's read: PEACE FOR REESE.

"Hey, our slogans are almost the same," Stephanie pointed out as Max held his sign up.

Max looked into her eyes and grinned. "Great minds think alike," he declared.

Stephanie felt her heart begin to beat faster. Max was looking at her as if he *liked* her. "Yeah, I guess we make a pretty good team," she replied.

A pretty great *team*, she added silently.

"They're here!" Uncle Tim cried. "The city council!"

Max turned away from Stephanie and pointed to the city council members. They walked through the crowd and up the steps leading to the council building.

"It's time, Steph," Max cried. He waved his sign high in the air. "Leave Reese in Peace!" he began chanting.

"Leave Reese in Peace!" Stephanie repeated.

Soon the whole crowd was holding up signs and shouting. "Leave Reese in Peace! Leave Reese in Peace!"

"Come on—we have to go inside," Max said when the council members disappeared into the building. "Let's go, everybody!" he cried, waving to the rest of the demonstrators.

He grabbed Stephanie's hand and pulled her up the stairs to the council building.

I can't believe it, Stephanie thought happily. *Max is holding my hand! We're holding hands just like a boyfriend and girlfriend.*

"Steph!" a voice called through the crowd. Stephanie gasped. Darcy!

Quickly, Stephanie pulled her hand out of Max's grasp. *What if Darcy saw us holding hands?* she thought. *She would be so mad at me. She's supposed to be Max's girlfriend, not me.*

"Steph, I'm so sorry about the signs," Darcy cried, pushing her way through a group of demonstrators to stand with Stephanie and Max.

"Don't worry about it—" Stephanie began.

"Hey, Darcy!" Max interrupted. "I'm glad you made it."

116

Darcy smiled at him. "So am I."

Stephanie's heart sank. Max and Darcy seemed to be getting more comfortable with each other. Darcy didn't even look nervous about talking to him.

I have to stop thinking like this, Stephanie told herself. *Max and Darcy like each other. Sure, Max held my hand—but it didn't mean anything to him.*

He thinks of me only as a friend.

"Let's go," Max said. He followed the council members into the big room where they held their meetings. The council took their seats at a long table at the front of the room. The demonstrators sat in seats in the audience.

Stephanie sat next to Max in the front row. Darcy took a seat on his other side. Stephanie turned around and spotted her family sitting with Allie toward the back of the room.

"Quiet, please!" called the council president, a tall woman with short, dark hair. She wore a navy blue suit and horn-rimmed glasses. "We need to get this meeting started so that we can address your concerns."

Once the room was quiet, the president spoke again. "We need one spokesperson. Who's the leader of this group?"

Dozens of fingers pointed to Max.

His freckled face flushed red as all eyes in the

room turned on him. Then he tightened his tie and stood up. "I am," Max announced.

The president looked down at Max over the top of her glasses. "You're a little young to be leading such a big group, aren't you?" she asked. The other council members chuckled.

Max stepped forward, closer to the council members. "I'm young. But most of the people who need Reese Park are even younger than I am," he replied.

Max waved some of the Reese Park neighborhood kids forward. They stood up and surrounded him. Stephanie noticed Nicky and Alex near the front, holding hands.

"Don't these kids deserve a park to play in?" Max asked the council. "Don't they deserve a place to ride their bikes? To play tag or softball? To have a picnic with their families?"

The room was silent. The council members stared at Max, hanging on every word.

"The park has been neglected for a long time," Max pointed out. "But we've done a lot of work there already. And we want to do more. We want to make Reese Park as beautiful as it used to be—if you'll only give us the chance. Right?" Max asked, turning to the crowd.

"Right! Right!" the demonstrators cheered loudly.

"Thank you," the president said. "You can sit down now."

Max sank into the chair next to Stephanie with a sigh. "Whew," he whispered, wiping his forehead with the back of his hand. "That was rough."

"What a speech!" Stephanie whispered back. "You were great!"

"Amazing," Darcy agreed.

Max smiled at her.

"Would anyone else like to speak?" the president asked.

"I would," a familiar voice called out.

"That's my father!" Stephanie told Max, turning around to watch Danny rise from his seat and walk to the front of the room.

"Parks are so precious," Danny began. "Without them, my children would have no place to run, no place to swing on a swing, and maybe no place to dream. These young people have worked hard to figure out how to make Reese Park a place to play again. And I can't think of a better way to spend our money than on our children. Can you?"

After Danny, eight more adults stood up and spoke to the council. After about an hour of speeches, the council members had a short discussion among themselves. Then the president banged her gavel for attention.

"Those were stirring speeches," she said. Then she stared at Max. "We're very impressed with the community support you've gathered. In fact, we're so impressed with your plans for the cleanup that we'll give in to your request. We're not going to sell the park land."

A loud, happy roar went up in the room.

The council president banged her gavel again. "Quiet!"

Once the noise had stopped, she continued. "We're also going to donate a Dumpster for the cleanup effort. And give you fifty bushes to plant!"

Another loud cheer rang out.

"We won!" Stephanie cried. "We did it!" She turned to congratulate Max.

"Max, this is so . . ." Stephanie started.

But she stopped in mid-sentence.

Darcy was planting a kiss on Max's cheek. Max was holding her hand. Then Darcy grinned at Max proudly. And Max grinned right back.

Stephanie felt a lump form in her throat.

All of a sudden Stephanie didn't feel happy about Reese Park. She didn't feel happy about *anything*.

I can't stop liking Max, she realized. *I can't stop liking him no matter how much I want to.*

I found a great guy. A guy who's perfect for me. A guy who cares about the same things that I do.

But I gave him away. To my best friend.

Chapter
12

◆ ◀ ◆ ◆

"Max, that was so awesome!" Darcy cried.

Stephanie couldn't stand hearing Max and Darcy talk to each other. She couldn't stand seeing them smile at each other. It hurt too much.

I have to get out of here, Stephanie thought, jumping to her feet. She ran past Darcy and Max toward the back of the room.

"Steph, where are you going?" Michelle cried as Stephanie dashed past her family and out of the council building.

She didn't answer.

Stephanie hurried into the parking lot and yanked open the door of the Tanners' station wagon. She slumped into the front seat and rested her head on the padded steering wheel.

How could I do this? How could I like Max? Stephanie thought miserably. *Why did I let myself like him, when I knew Darcy liked him?*

Max and I get along so well. We belong together, she thought. *But that can never happen. How could I even want it to? I'm a terrible person. And I'm a terrible best friend.*

Stephanie heard a light tapping sound. She lifted her head—and saw Danny peering through the car window. He pulled open the passenger side door. "Mind if I sit down?" he asked in a gentle voice.

Stephanie shook her head.

"You okay?" Danny asked.

Stephanie shook her head again.

"Want to talk about it?" Danny asked.

"I'm a horrible, awful person," she burst out, wiping away a tear that trickled down her face. "The worst."

Danny frowned. "I've never known you to be horrible or awful," he said.

"But I am," Stephanie sniffled. "And it's all Cyrano's fault."

Danny wrinkled his nose in confusion. "Cyrano?" he asked. "As in Cyrano de Bergerac— from the play?"

Stephanie nodded. "We were reading *Cyrano* and Darcy couldn't talk to Max, so I wrote notes to him and I pretended I was her. And now I like him, and he likes Darcy. And Darcy thinks she likes him, but it's all wrong. They can hardly even talk to each other! And now I can't go to cleanup day or the party afterward. It would hurt too much!"

"Whoa! Slow down!" Danny cried. "You're not terrible or horrible," he said kindly. "You were trying to be a good friend by writing those notes. You thought you were helping Darcy."

Stephanie nodded.

"But your notes made Max think Darcy is something that she isn't—some*one* that she isn't."

"I know!" Stephanie said. "My notes made it seem as if Darcy is interested in the things *I* like. But Darcy isn't like me at all!"

"Well, now Darcy and Max have to figure that out for themselves," Danny said.

"But what am I supposed to do about liking Max?" Stephanie asked. "How could I do that to Darcy? I'm her best friend!"

"You're not wrong for liking Max," he replied. "You couldn't help that. And I know it hurts to be around them. But you put so much into this park project—it would be wrong of you not to go to the cleanup day or the party. It's really *your* project too."

Stephanie thought for a moment. "I don't know about going to the party. But I'd really hate to miss the big cleanup day," she admitted. She sighed. "Okay, I'll go to the cleanup. But I won't have any fun."

"Come on, what could be more fun than a cleanup?" Danny asked.

Stephanie couldn't help laughing. Her dad would definitely have fun if there was cleaning involved!

"There's one more thing I think you should do," Danny added. "I think you should be honest with Darcy."

"You mean *tell* Darcy that I like Max?" Stephanie cried. "No way! I can't tell her how I really feel. She would never forgive me."

Maybe Darcy will have to meet with her hockey coach at lunch, Stephanie thought, dragging her feet as she walked toward the cafeteria on Friday.

She had avoided talking to Darcy all morning. She knew her friend would want to tell her all about Max.

And Stephanie just didn't want to hear about Darcy's perfect romance with the boy *she* liked.

But I can't avoid Darcy forever, Stephanie realized. *She's my best friend. I just have to get it over with.*

Stephanie bought her lunch—a grilled cheese sandwich with extra tomato—and carried her tray to the usual table near the window. Darcy and Allie were already munching as Stephanie sat down.

"Hey, you missed it last night," Darcy said, looking up from her double pizza bagel. "We went for sodas after the demonstration. Where did you disappear to?"

"Yeah," Allie piped up. "I turned around and you were running out the door. Where did you go?"

"Nowhere," Stephanie replied, staring at her grilled cheese.

"Well, I had a date," Darcy declared. "Sort of. Max came with us for sodas. So did Paul."

Stephanie looked up and tried to smile at her friend. She noticed Allie watching her carefully.

"Darcy, that's . . . really nice," she said weakly.

Darcy frowned. "Actually, it was kind of weird," she replied. "I like Max so, so much. I mean, he's the cutest guy I've ever seen. But last night we barely had anything to say to each other."

126

Stephanie glanced at Allie. Allie nodded, as if to say that Darcy was telling the truth.

Darcy played with the straw in her milk container. "His notes are so cool. But in person . . . nothing works out right," she continued. "Max didn't tell any jokes, like he does in his notes. Half the time, I didn't even really know what he was talking about."

She gazed at Stephanie with a puzzled frown on her face. "What was in those notes you wrote to Max anyway?"

Stephanie stared at her friend in shock, nearly dropping her grilled cheese. "What do you mean, what was in the notes?" she cried. "Didn't you read them?"

"I meant to." Darcy gave Stephanie a small, guilty smile. "But I know what a good writer you are, so I knew you'd do a great job. And you know how busy I've been with the hockey team and all."

This can't be true, Stephanie thought angrily. *I spent hours writing notes to Max, trying to make each one absolutely perfect. And Darcy never even bothered to read them!*

Max really likes her, all because of my notes. And she doesn't even know what they say!

"Tell me what to do, Steph," Darcy cried. "Tell me what I'm supposed to say to him. I like Max *so* much! But this whole thing just doesn't work when Max and I have to talk to each other."

Stephanie leapt to her feet. She couldn't keep her feelings inside anymore. "That's because *you* like Max only because he's cute!" she blurted out. "But I like the real Max—the whole person, not just the way he looks!"

Darcy gasped. "What?" she cried. "What do you mean, *you* like Max?"

Allie put down her sandwich. "Listen, guys . . ." she started.

But Darcy ignored her. She jumped from her seat and faced Stephanie. "You like Max?" she shouted, her dark eyes flashing. "How could you?"

"Because that's not you in the notes I've been writing. It's me!" Stephanie declared. "All I've been doing is making excuses for you. And I want to tell Max the truth—all of it!"

"You wouldn't dare!" Darcy replied angrily. "Boy, Stephanie, I thought you were my friend. How could you go behind my back like this?"

Darcy grabbed her lunch tray, turned, and stalked off.

"Ohhhhhh," Allie murmured. "That was . . . ohhhhhh."

Stephanie sank back into her seat. Her hands were shaking, and she felt like crying.

I really messed things up, she thought. *I found a boy I really like—and I gave him away.*

I don't have Max. And now I don't have Darcy either.

CHAPTER
13

"Can Allie and I get out here?" Stephanie asked on Saturday morning.

Danny had just pulled up at the entrance to Reese Park. From the car window, Stephanie could see dozens of kids and grown-ups already making their way into the park for the big cleanup.

She felt too nervous to even wait for Danny to pull into the parking lot. She couldn't wait to see Max and tell him the truth—that she was the one who wrote all the letters.

"Can I go with Stephanie?" Michelle asked.

"Sure," Danny replied. "We'll see you inside."

Stephanie, Allie, and Michelle piled out of the station wagon. "Stephanie, did I show you my autographed book?" Michelle asked as they hurried into the park.

"Huh?" Stephanie muttered. She glanced around, looking for Max.

"D.J. got Grace Farrell to sign a book for me," Michelle cried. "Isn't that cool?"

"Yeah, I guess," Stephanie said.

"And she told Grace Farrell about me forging a note from Dad, and Ms. Farrell said she was going to use that story in a Mary Mosley book!"

"Umm-hmm," Stephanie answered. She was barely listening to her sister. All she could think about was talking to Max.

"Hey, Steph, there he is," Allie said, pointing across the field toward the banks of the pond.

Stephanie squinted in that direction. She could see a big group of adults and kids standing on the banks. One wore a red bandanna. Max.

Stephanie felt her heart begin to pound as she, Allie, and Michelle made their way toward the group. "I don't know, Allie," she whispered. "Now that I see Max, I don't know if I can actually tell him the truth. I feel as tongue-tied as Darcy did."

"Come on," Allie urged her. "You never had trouble talking to Max before."

"I know, but I'm nervous. What if Max really likes Darcy? What if he still likes *her* even after I tell him the truth?"

Allie gave her a sympathetic smile. "You'll never find out unless you talk to him."

As they got closer, Stephanie could see Max pulling garbage bags from a box and handing them out to the volunteers. Paul, standing next to Max, was handing out work gloves to everyone.

Max looked really cute—and really happy to be working on the cleanup. *This is the day he's been waiting for,* Stephanie thought.

And it's a day he'll want to share with Darcy.

Stephanie felt sick to her stomach. She hung back a little as Allie and Michelle continued walking toward the group.

"Aren't you coming, Steph?" Michelle asked.

Stephanie shrugged.

"Do you want me to get you a garbage bag and gloves?" Allie asked. Her green eyes were worried.

Stephanie nodded. *She understands,* Stephanie thought. *Thank goodness I have one best friend left.*

"Thanks," Stephanie said. "I want to tell him about the notes. But I just can't talk to him now,

Allie. I can't—I'm too afraid that he won't like me."

As Allie hurried over to Max, Stephanie turned to Michelle. Her little sister was staring at her with a strange expression on her face. A *determined* expression.

"You must be *really* sad about Max," Michelle said. "You don't even want to see my autographed book."

Stephanie smiled a little. "Sorry, Michelle," she said. "I'll look at it later, okay?"

Michelle was still giving her that strange look. "I have to go, um, do something, Steph," she announced. "It's really important."

"Uh-huh," Stephanie murmured. She watched as Max talked to Allie.

"I'll be back soon," Michelle added.

"Okay," Stephanie replied. Max was laughing as he handed a bunch of garbage bags to Allie.

Stephanie wished she were over there, laughing with Max.

Michelle walked off toward the swing sets. Allie returned with a pile of garbage bags and work gloves. "Max wants us to hand these out as new people come," she explained as she placed the bags and gloves on the ground next to Stephanie.

The two friends picked up bags for themselves and began filling them with garbage. In a moment the rest of Stephanie's family arrived and began working too.

"Darcy's here," Allie declared a few minutes later, motioning toward the street with her head.

Stephanie glanced up. Darcy, wearing bright purple overalls, walked into Reese Park, followed by about a dozen kids. All of them were members of the hockey, tennis, and lacrosse teams.

Stephanie felt her stomach drop as Darcy drew closer.

"Hi!" Darcy exclaimed, staring past Stephanie and right at Allie. "I brought the gang with me. What should we do?"

I guess Darcy's not talking to me, Stephanie thought, tossing a handful of trash into her bag.

Suddenly she felt angry.

Fine. Then I won't talk to Darcy either, she decided. *If Darcy were a good best friend, she would understand that I didn't start liking Max on purpose.*

There was silence for a moment as Allie waited for Stephanie to answer Darcy's question.

"Oh! Well, there are bags and work gloves there—next to Stephanie," Allie finally said.

"Stephanie? I don't have any friends named Stephanie," Darcy replied.

Oh, please, Stephanie thought. "Allie, tell the person in the purple overalls that she can pick up garbage on the other side of the field. As far away as possible!" Stephanie snapped.

"Allie, please tell the person in the faded-out jeans that I'll clean up wherever I want to. And I think I'll clean up right here!" Darcy replied as she slid the work gloves on her hands.

Allie sighed, picked up a plastic container, and threw it into her bag.

I'm just going to ignore Darcy, Stephanie thought as she crammed some rusty old jar tops into her garbage bag.

Darcy, standing next to Allie, stooped down and quickly began scooping big armfuls of junk into her bag—as if she were determined to clean up more garbage than Stephanie.

"Working hard?" a voice called out.

Max! Without thinking, Stephanie began to answer him. "Hardly work—" she started.

Then she stopped. Max was talking to Darcy. Not to her.

Out of the corner of her eye Stephanie saw Darcy smile at Max. "Working very hard," she declared. "Look—practically a full garbage bag already!"

Stephanie felt like putting her hands over her ears. *I can't stand listening to Max and Darcy talk to each other,* she thought. *Especially when he thinks that Darcy is someone she isn't.*

He thinks that she is me!

I have to tell Max the truth, Stephanie thought. *As soon as I work up the courage to do it.*

For the rest of the long day, Stephanie tried her best to stay away from Darcy and Max. Just keep busy, she told herself.

First she filled about ten bags with junk and tossed them into the huge dumpster on the sidewalk. Then she helped Becky, Michelle, and the twins plant red and white begonias in a heart-shaped plot in the middle of the park. After that Stephanie worked with Jesse, D.J., Allie, and Joey pulling trash out of the pond.

"Keep an eye on your dad," Joey joked to Stephanie. He nodded toward Danny on the other side of the park. "I think he's going to try to clean the Dumpster next!"

Late in the afternoon, Stephanie sneaked a peek at Max. He stood on a ladder tossing garbage bags into the almost-full Dumpster. His blond hair hung limply in his eyes. And his white T-shirt was covered with dirt.

I have to tell him that I'm the one who wrote those notes, she thought for the millionth time. *I just have to come right out and say it:* "Max, I'm Mystery Girl. Not Darcy, *me*."

Stephanie could imagine Max's response. At first he would be confused. But when he realized what had happened, when he realized that Stephanie was the girl in the notes . . .

He'll be furious, Stephanie thought. *He'll think I lied to him. He'll be so mad at both me and Darcy that he'll never speak to either of us again.*

Stephanie knew she still had to tell Max the truth. But how could she get the words out, when she knew it might make him hate her forever?

As Stephanie watched, Max cupped his hands around his mouth like a megaphone. "Time to quit!" he shouted. "You guys did an amazing job. This place looks fantastic! Everybody, stop and look around."

Stephanie gazed around Reese Park. The afternoon sun cast a peaceful glow over the neatly mowed grass. The pond's banks were free of garbage, and the water shone a clear blue. Tons of bright flowers and bushy seedlings were planted throughout the park. And in the middle of it all was a fantastic playground, with swings, seesaws, and slides.

"It's beautiful," Stephanie declared to Allie. "Really, really beautiful."

Danny and Michelle walked up to Stephanie. "We did some job," Danny said proudly. "And you kids organized the entire thing. I'm proud of you."

Stephanie smiled at her father. She felt so good about the park that she almost forgot to be sad about the Max-and-Darcy situation. Almost.

"Now I can ride my bike here with Cassie and Mandy," Michelle said happily. Cassie and Mandy were her two best friends. "And Nicky and Alex can play here when they're older."

"Michelle, let's go find the others," Danny suggested.

"I want to stay with Stephanie," Michelle protested.

Stephanie shrugged. "Sure," she said.

As Danny walked away, Stephanie spotted Max and Paul heading in her direction. "Oh, no, Michelle, there's Max," Stephanie told her little sister. "And he's coming this way!"

"He looks weird," Michelle said. "Upset or something."

Max did look upset, with a frown wrinkling his brow. He walked straight up to Stephanie and gazed into her eyes.

"Stephanie, I've been looking everywhere for

you," Max declared with a serious expression. "I have something important to tell you."

Stephanie gulped. *It's now or never,* she thought.

"And I have something really important to tell you," she told Max.

CHAPTER
14

◆ ◂ ◆ ◆

Stephanie opened her mouth to speak. But before she could utter a word, Max pulled a folded piece of paper from his jeans pocket.

"Look at this," Max exclaimed, holding the paper in front of Stephanie's eyes.

Stephanie read the words on the paper.

Dear Max,

You should know that Stephanie really likes you. A lot. Stephanie is a great person, and I think you should like her. Not me.

Darcy Powell

"What's going on, Steph?" Max asked. "The handwriting isn't like any of Darcy's other notes. And why did Darcy sign her last name?"

Stephanie inhaled sharply, her heart pounding like a drum. "I-I don't know," she stammered. "This isn't Darcy's handwriting."

Even as she said the words, Stephanie realized exactly who had written the mortifying note.

"Michelle!" she cried, turning to her sister. "Did you do this? Did you write this note and sign Darcy's name?"

Michelle grinned. "Yup," she said proudly, not realizing how embarrassed Stephanie was. "You said I shouldn't use Dad's handwriting anymore—but you didn't say not to use Darcy's."

Stephanie felt herself blush from her face to her feet. *I can't believe this is happening*, she thought. *I can't believe Michelle told Max that I like him!*

"Michelle!" Stephanie yelled. "I told you never to forge notes—I told you it was wrong!"

Michelle frowned. "You said I shouldn't forge a note just to get something I wanted. But I didn't—I wrote this note for *you!*"

"But I didn't ask you to! Michelle, you're in big trouble!" Stephanie declared.

"Why? I was just trying to help!" Michelle cried. "I saw *you* write all those notes for Darcy!"

"Wait a second—*you* wrote the notes, Stephanie?" Max cried.

"Stephanie!" a voice gasped. "How could you?"

Stephanie whirled around. Darcy stood behind her, her face flaming red. She must have heard what Max said.

This is awful, Stephanie thought. *This is the worst thing that ever happened to me.*

Max and Paul stood watching her with confused expressions. Michelle looked ready to cry. And Darcy's eyes flashed with anger.

"You wrote the notes, all right," Darcy snapped. "But why did you have to tell Max everything?"

"Wait—no," Stephanie started. "I didn't tell—"

Darcy cut her off. "Okay, Max, so now you know," she declared. "Stephanie wrote all the notes to you, not me."

Darcy took a deep breath. "You made me so nervous that I couldn't even talk to you," she told Max, her voice high and her words coming out faster and faster. "And we were reading *Cyrano de Bergerac* in class, and that gave me the idea to have Stephanie write you notes. So now you know what a stupid phony I am," she finished.

Max and Paul stood staring at Darcy, their mouths hanging open in amazement.

Then Max turned back to Stephanie. "*You* wrote them?" Max asked her. "Those notes in my locker?"

Stephanie nodded. Darcy stared at the ground, embarrassed.

This is not *the way I wanted Max to find out the truth,* Stephanie thought. *He must think Darcy and I are nuts. He must think my entire family is nuts.*

And then Max and Paul burst out laughing.

What's going on? Stephanie thought in confusion. *What's so funny?* She glanced at Darcy, and saw her friend frowning as well.

But Max and Paul just kept laughing.

"What's so funny?" Darcy demanded.

Max gulped, trying to contain his laughter. "Well, you might not know it, but I'm pretty shy myself—at least around girls," he explained. "And we were reading *Cyrano* in class too. So when I got Mystery Girl's note, we got the idea for Paul to sort of, um, *help* me with my answers."

"What do you mean, *help* you?" Stephanie asked.

Max laughed again. "Well, those were Paul's notes—and his corny jokes—in Darcy's locker," he explained.

Suddenly the whole situation started to seem funny.

"I can't believe this," Stephanie cried. She turned to Darcy. "We weren't the only ones faking the notes."

She began to giggle, thinking of Paul writing Max's notes and slipping them into Darcy's locker.

Even Darcy cracked a small smile. Then she began to chuckle.

In a moment, all four of them were doubled over with laughter.

"Your jokes, huh?" Darcy asked Paul between giggles.

He nodded. "Pretty bad, aren't they?" he asked.

Darcy laughed. "No worse than mine," she replied.

"Hey, I've got millions of bad jokes," Paul said with a smile. "Want to hear a few?"

"Yeah, I do," Darcy declared. She and Paul looked into each other's eyes and laughed.

Max turned to Stephanie. "So you're the real Mystery Girl," he said.

Stephanie grinned. "I guess so," she replied.

"Maybe I should call you Cyrano—or Cyranette," he teased.

"I don't know . . . Mad Max," Stephanie teased back.

Max smiled shyly. "Maybe I'll just call you Stephanie," he said. "As long as I can *call* you— you know, to go out for pizza or a movie. Can I?"

"Definitely!" Stephanie answered.

Max's eyes lit up. "Great! You know, I've wanted to call you for a while—ever since we started working together on the cleanup. But then I got those notes from Darcy—I mean from you—and, well, I got confused. I didn't know *who* to like!"

"Now you know," Stephanie told him.

Max gave her a warm smile. "Maybe we could dance. You do dance, don't you? And you did bring those tapes, right?" Max asked.

"Yes to both questions," Stephanie answered. She held up the blue canvas bag. "The tapes are right here."

"Great." Max smiled. "I'll go put them in the tape deck. Be back in two minutes."

Stephanie watched happily as Max walked toward the stage. Darcy and Paul were deep in conversation, laughing what seemed like every five seconds. *They're really hitting it off,* Stephanie thought.

"Do you guys want sodas?" Paul asked.

"Yes!" Darcy and Stephanie replied at once.

As Paul walked off, Stephanie glanced at Darcy. She couldn't tell what her former best friend was thinking.

Stephanie gave Darcy a small smile. Darcy bit her lip, then smiled back. In a minute they were both laughing again.

"What's so funny?" Michelle demanded.

Stephanie and Darcy turned in surprise. Stephanie had forgotten all about Michelle.

Michelle glared at her. "How come you yelled at *me* for forging notes, but you think it's funny when Paul forged notes from Max?" she asked Stephanie.

"Oh, Michelle," Stephanie said. "I'm sorry I yelled. But you embarrassed me."

"Anyway," Darcy put in. "You should never, ever pretend to be someone you aren't, Michelle. That's what got us all into trouble in the first place."

Michelle shook her head. "Don't worry. From now on I'm writing notes only in my own handwriting, from *me!* I don't ever want to get as confused as you all are!"

She stomped away.

Stephanie grinned at Darcy. "Well, at least *she* learned her lesson," she joked. "But so did I,

146

Darce. I shouldn't have written those notes. I shouldn't have pretended to be you."

"It's not just that, Steph," Darcy said. "You should have told me right away that you liked Max. You should have been honest with me."

Stephanie raised an eyebrow. "Honest?" she asked. "Excuse me, who was pretending that my notes were hers?"

Darcy grinned. "Good point," she admitted. "I guess I was upset because you got along with Max better than I did. Max and I—we really didn't click. I had such a big crush on him, but I guess that didn't mean we were right for each other."

"Maybe not," Stephanie agreed.

"You know, I think I liked the *idea* of liking Max more than I liked Max!" Darcy said. "Does that make sense?"

"I think so," Stephanie replied. "But you and Paul get along really great," she pointed out.

Darcy nodded. "Yeah, he's funny—and he writes a mean note!" she exclaimed. "Plus, he dared me to try to beat him in tennis. Wait till he sees my backhand. And, Steph?"

"Yeah?" Stephanie asked.

"It's okay that you like Max," Darcy said. "I mean, I like Paul. He's really the one I liked all along, I guess. He's the boy from the funny notes."

Stephanie smiled at her best friend. "Thanks, Darce. I wouldn't know what to do without you," she said.

Darcy nodded. "Me either."

Stephanie hugged her best friend. "Come on," Darcy said. "Let's party! Now we really have something to celebrate."

FULL HOUSE
Stephanie ™

PHONE CALL FROM A FLAMINGO	88004-7/$3.99
THE BOY-OH-BOY NEXT DOOR	88121-3/$3.99
TWIN TROUBLES	88290-2/$3.99
HIP HOP TILL YOU DROP	88291-0/$3.99
HERE COMES THE BRAND NEW ME	89858-2/$3.99
THE SECRET'S OUT	89859-0/$3.99
DADDY'S NOT-SO-LITTLE GIRL	89860-4/$3.99
P.S. FRIENDS FOREVER	89861-2/$3.99
GETTING EVEN WITH THE FLAMINGOES	52273-6/$3.99
THE DUDE OF MY DREAMS	52274-4/$3.99
BACK-TO-SCHOOL COOL	52275-2/$3.99
PICTURE ME FAMOUS	52276-0/$3.99
TWO-FOR-ONE CHRISTMAS FUN	53546-3/$3.99
THE BIG FIX-UP MIX-UP	53547-1/$3.99
TEN WAYS TO WRECK A DATE	53548-X/$3.99
WISH UPON A VCR	53549-8/$3.99
DOUBLES OR NOTHING	56841-8/$3.99
SUGAR AND SPICE ADVICE	56842-6/$3.99
NEVER TRUST A FLAMINGO	56843-4/$3.99
THE TRUTH ABOUT BOYS	00361-5/$3.99
CRAZY ABOUT THE FUTURE	00362-3/$3.99
MY SECRET ADMIRER	00363-1/$3.99

Available from Minstrel® Books Published by Pocket Books

FULL HOUSE™
Michelle

#1: THE GREAT PET PROJECT 51905-0/$3.50
#2: THE SUPER-DUPER SLEEPOVER PARTY
       51906-9/$3.50
#3: MY TWO BEST FRIENDS 52271-X/$3.99
#4: LUCKY, LUCKY DAY 52272-8/$3.50
#5: THE GHOST IN MY CLOSET 53573-0/$3.99
#6: BALLET SURPRISE 53574-9/$3.99
#7: MAJOR LEAGUE TROUBLE 53575-7/$3.99
#8: MY FOURTH-GRADE MESS 53576-5/$3.99
#9: BUNK 3, TEDDY, AND ME 56834-5/$3.99
#10: MY BEST FRIEND IS A MOVIE STAR!
       (Super Edition) 56835-3/$3.99
#11: THE BIG TURKEY ESCAPE 56836-1/$3.99
#12: THE SUBSTITUTE TEACHER 00364-X/$3.99
#13: CALLING ALL PLANETS 00365-8/$3.99
#14: I'VE GOT A SECRET 00366-6/$3.99
#15: HOW TO BE COOL 00833-1/$3.99
#16: THE NOT-SO-GREAT OUTDOORS 00835-8/$3.99

A MINSTREL® BOOK

Published by Pocket Books

Simon & Schuster Mail Order Dept. BWB
200 Old Tappan Rd., Old Tappan, N.J. 07675

Please send me the books I have checked above. I am enclosing $_____ (please add $0.75 to cover the
postage and handling for each order. Please add appropriate sales tax). Send check or money order--no cash
or C.O.D.'s please. Allow up to six weeks for delivery. For purchase over $10.00 you may use VISA: card
number, expiration date and customer signature must be included.

Name _____

Address _____

City _____ State/Zip _____

VISA Card # _____ Exp.Date _____

Signature _____

1033-20

It doesn't matter if you live around the corner...
or around the world...
If you are a fan of Mary-Kate and Ashley Olsen,
you should be a member of

MARY-KATE + ASHLEY'S FUN CLUB™

Here's what you get:
Our Funzine™
An autographed color photo
Two black & white individual photos
A full size color poster
An official **Fun Club**™ membership card
A **Fun Club**™ school folder
Two special **Fun Club**™ surprises
A holiday card
Fun Club™ collectibles catalog
Plus a **Fun Club**™ box to keep everything in

To join Mary-Kate + Ashley's Fun Club™, fill out the form
below and send it along with

U.S. Residents – $17.00
Canadian Residents – $22 U.S. Funds
International Residents – $27 U.S. Funds

MARY-KATE + ASHLEY'S FUN CLUB™
859 HOLLYWOOD WAY, SUITE 275
BURBANK, CA 91505

NAME:_____

ADDRESS:_____

_CITY:_____ STATE:_____ ZIP:_____

PHONE:(____) _____ BIRTHDATE:_____

TM & © 1996 Dualstar Entertainment Group, Inc.

1242